How ~~~

indebted to the vampires

ERIN BEDFORD

Indebted to the Vampires © 2018-24
Embrace the Fantasy Publishing, LLC

All rights reserved under the International and Pan-American Copyright Conventions. No part of this book may be reproduced or transmitted in any form or by any means, electronic or mechanical, including photocopying, recording, or by any information storage and retrieval system, without permission in writing from the publisher.

This is a work of fiction. Names, places, characters and incidents are either the product of the author's imagination or are used fictitiously, and any resemblance to any actual persons, living or dead, organizations, events or locales is entirely coincidental.

Warning: the unauthorized reproduction or distribution of this copyrighted work is illegal. Criminal copyright infringement, including infringement without monetary gain, is investigated by the FBI and is punishable by up to 5 years in prison and a fine of $250,000.

ALSO BY ERIN BEDFORD

The Underground Series
Chasing Rabbits
Chasing Cats
Chasing Princes
Chasing Shadows
Chasing Hearts
The Crimes of Alice

The Mary Wiles Chronicles
Marked by Hell
Bound by Hell
Deceived by Hell
Tempted by Hell

Starcrossed Dragons
Riding Lightning
Grinding Frost
Swallowing Fire
Pounding Earth

The Celestial War Chronicles
Song of Blood and Fire

The Crimson Fold
Until Midnight
Until Dawn
Until Sunset
Until Twilight

Curse of the Fairy Tales
Rapunzel Untamed
Rapunzel Unveiled

Her Angels
Heaven's Embrace
Heaven's A Beach
Heaven's Most Wanted

Academy of Witches
Witching On A Star
As You Witch
Witch You Were Here

Granting Her Wish
Vampire CEO

House of Durand 1

ERIN BEDFORD

CHAPTER 1

Piper

I CAN'T BELIEVE I got talked into this, I thought for the millionth time since I left the house. So, what if I'm in between jobs right now? That doesn't mean that I'll take whatever the temp agency will throw at me.

"It's not like I didn't have other offers," I muttered to myself as I turned down the road toward my new place of work. "Sure, all those offers were for jobs I wouldn't do even if I was starving, but that didn't mean I wanted to be someone's maid."

My words trailed off as I pulled into the driveway of my assigned house. A wrought iron fence wrapped around the entire premises with an intercom box at the gate entrance. I could barely see the brick mansion behind the gate between the large hedges doing their best to block my view.

That wasn't promising. With my luck, I was going to be saddled with some grumpy old shut-in who would hover over my every movement.

"Can I help you?" an annoyed voice barked out of the intercom, making me jump.

The fact that I had heard the voice even through my closed window did not make me feel any better about this job. It was getting even more certain that my new boss was a wrinkly old geezer with too much time on their hands which meant they'd have plenty of time to harp at me.

Quickly rolling the window down, I stuttered, "Um, yeah, hi. I'm Piper. Piper Billings. The agency sent me." I paused and then added, "To, uh, clean."

Smooth. Real smooth. Already off to a great start.

The voice didn't answer back, but a buzz sounded, and the gates opened before me at a glacial pace. Grandpa pace.

I shouted toward the box, "Thank you!" then inched my way into the circular driveway.

Now that the gate was out of the way, I could see the brick mansion in its entirety. Large columns held a roof over the porch where two black double doors stood looming before me. All the windows in the house were covered by heavy drapes. I couldn't even peek into the house I would be working at for the next few months.

Shut in? Check.

I sat in my car, gaping at the house. Sure, I'd bitched and moaned about going from a cushy desk job with benefits, two weeks of vacation, and holiday pay to temporary work, but I never imagined I'd end up working in a place like this. I was a 'hide behind my business casual clothing, let's chitchat at the water cooler' kind of girl, not a 'uniform and manners required' kind of girl.

My family wasn't poor. I mean, I was, but that was because I sucked at saving money. However, never in my wildest dreams would I think I would ever have the chance to walk inside of a house like this, let alone work in it.

Even though I would be living in it, cleaning it would be a bitch, which more than put things in perspective.

Knock, knock, knock.

I jumped for the second time in my seat, my heart pounding in my chest as I turned to my driver side window. Now I was gaping for a whole other reason.

A handsome man in a suit with white gloves stood bent over, his hand held up as if to knock again. The impatient look in his eyes showed that he had definitely noticed me loitering out here.

My face flushed red. If I thought I had embarrassed myself before, being caught drooling over the front of the house just put another point against me.

I'd be out of points before I even made it through the front door.

Turning my car off, I grabbed my bag and quickly got out of the car. Standing next to the handsome man, I was dwarfed by his height. I smoothed a hand over my dress pants and cleared my throat before offering him my best professional smile.

"I'm sorry. I always get nervous on my first day." I let out a neurotic chuckle and tucked a strand of my blonde hair behind my ear.

The man's face was as straight as the slicked back black hair on his head. "This way, Miss Billings."

His tone held a no-nonsense sort of feel to it as if he'd scold me for daring to think of doing anything other than following him. Not that he waited to see if I was coming. He strode across the driveaway, his long legs carrying him into the house before I had time to process what had just happened.

What a stuck-up twat. I grumbled under my breath as I took my time entering the house. If he wasn't going to be nice, then he couldn't expect me to do the same.

All thoughts of pretending to be professional went out the window the moment I stepped into the house. With my mouth falling open once more, I stared up at the walls around me.

The foyer had vaulted ceilings with a shiny chandelier filling the room with artificial light. Two sets of staircases sat on either side of the room, and a balcony off the second floor could be seen from the ground. The runner carpet covering the front area had to cost a fortune with its crimson color and gold inlay, not to forget the pieces of art decorating the walls and side tables.

If I hadn't been nervous before, I was now.

I wasn't what anyone would call graceful. Okay, I was a klutz, a 'Murphy hates me, stay away from anything so much as a fork' kind of klutz.

Don't believe me?

Okay, I once broke a bone in a bouncy house. Yes. True story. How does one break a bone in something literally filled with air?

For me? Easy.

I'd been told I was a walking insurance claim waiting to happen. Something that made me think I should just turn right around now and save everyone the trouble.

Except I needed the money. Desperately.

By the time I stopped gawking at all the breakable things around me, I'd already lost my guide. My eyes darted around the room looking for the severely-in-need-of-a-blow-job guide, but he was nowhere to be found.

Taking a chance, I decided to go through an archway to the left which led into what looked like a living room. This room was even worse than the last one!

Unlike my home, there was no television, and the only entertaining thing was the large portrait of a couple who looked to be right out of a cliché horror movie. A severe expression marred both of their features, and their eyes seemed to watch me with every step which was easy to see from where it sat above a large fireplace, surrounded by a few dark maroon couches and chairs.

As I looked around and noticed my guide was nowhere in view, my eyes went down to the carpet. It was an oriental style rug that covered the sitting area in creams and dark reds to match the couch, except there was one spot on the carpet that was out of place. I knelt and rubbed my finger over the brown spot. Rough to the touch, it seemed to have dried on a while ago.

That's going to be tough to get out.

Standing back up, I didn't notice someone else was in the room until a throat cleared. Startled, I spun around and came face to face with the most beautiful man I had ever seen, and 'man' would be putting it lightly. This guy was an Adonis, a god, someone I should fall to my knees and worship just for allowing me to be in the same room as him.

His dark hair fell over his piercing blue eyes, and an aristocratic nose filled his face. The top lip of his mouth was thin while the bottom one was full as if he had a permanent pout on his face. His scruffy jaw and relaxed form made him seem like he had just gotten out of bed, not to forget the button-up shirt he had left unbuttoned and flapping at his side as he moved toward me.

"Uh, hi." I waved weakly. Cursing myself, I cleared my throat and tried again. "I'm Piper. Piper Billings. I'm the new maid."

The man didn't answer me but watched me intently. His head cocked to the side as he inched closer, one languid foot in front of the other. Like a large cat prowling toward their prey, but not like any cat I'd ever seen.

My eyes trailed down from his face to his exposed muscles, and my mouth went dry.

Don't think about sex. Don't think about sex. I chanted my mantra over and over again in my mind as my eyes settled on the line of hair going into this mystery man's pants. I jerked my eyes back up to his and swallowed hard at the hungry expression on his face.

The expression was so intense that it scared me.

I stumbled backward and stuttered over my words, "I'm not sure who you think you are, but I better find my guide before I get fired. I really need this job, you know."

A small part of me hoped he'd claim to be my new boss and show me how I could keep my job. Oh, I could think of several wicked ways he and I could enjoy some time together.

What the fuck? Am I in a trashy romance novel?

I shook my head to clear it, but the man kept coming. I kept moving back, trying to put some distance between us, not that it helped any. Swallowing down my desire for the man, I stumbled over my feet. Catching myself before I knocked an expensive lamp over, I pivoted left.

My feet found the side of the stand before I noticed it was there. I tried to stop it from falling, I really did. I didn't care much about my own wellbeing, but if I broke something my very first day, I was going to get fired for sure.

However, for all my good intentions, there was nothing I could do. Down came the stand, the vase sitting on it, and me. The sound of the vase smashing into a dozen pieces made me wince, or maybe that was the shard of the vase that I had fallen on. Either way, it was painful.

Sprawled out on the floor, I glanced down at my bleeding hand and then to what had to be an expensive vase decimated on the ground. Well, there goes this job. I sighed and cursed myself for my clumsiness and my raging hormones.

"Here."

The beautiful man knelt before me and picked up my hand. With as much intensity as he had stared me earlier, he picked the pieces of the vase out of the wound and sat them on the antique coffee table. Each touch of his hand made my blood pump harder in my veins. An aching need pulsed between my thighs, and my nipples pushed against my white blouse.

Geeze Louise, get a hold of yourself. It's just a guy. A smoking hot guy but still, only flesh and blood.

"Ah," I gasped as he withdrew a particularly deep piece.

His blue eyes shot up from my hand, and a small smile tipped his lips, but he didn't say anything. Those piercing eyes made me squirm.

I forced myself to stay still while he worked, my heart pounding in my chest all the while. When he was done, all that was left was a small cut.

"There," he said. "It doesn't look quite as bad as before. Just a little blood."

I gaped at him as he smiled, flashing his unusually long canines at me. It took a moment before I realized I was staring.

I licked my lips, an action that did not go unnoticed by him, and nodded. "Yeah, it's fine. I just need a bandage." I let him help me to my feet and then turned to the broken vase. "I'm really sorry about that. I'll pay for it of course."

The man chuckled, a sound that I found myself eager to hear more of. "You have fifteen million dollars to spend on a Qing Dynasty vase? I thought you were a maid?"

I could feel my face pale at his words. "Fif-fifteen million? On a vase?" My eyes bulged from my head at the broken pieces on the ground.

Lifting one shoulder as if it weren't a big deal, the man grabbed my wrist and led me to the couch. "Here, have a seat. I'll get you something to bandage your hand with, and then we can figure out some kind of payment plan." He winked at me and then left out a door on the other side of the room.

I sat there for a moment, reveling in my mortification. Fifteen million dollars. Who the hell had that kind of money? And to spend it on something like a vase? One that you placed anywhere that it could get knocked over! Rich people. I would never understand them.

"There you are," the same annoyed voice from before growled at me. I shot to my feet to meet my guide's vexed gaze.

My guide's brown eyes widened as he took in my bleeding hand and the broken pieces on the floor. "What the hell happened here?"

I winced. "I tripped?"

CHAPTER 2

Piper

APPARENTLY, THAT WAS NOT the right answer. My guide, who had yet to introduce himself, glared at me. He didn't seem to particularly care about the fact that I was bleeding. He only seemed to care that I had caused a disturbance after only five minutes in the house.

Can you blame him? No. Not really. I'd have thrown me out before I ever had the chance to break anything.

"Come on, you're done." He grabbed my arm and pulled me to my feet, seemingly determined to get me out of the house.

"But– but you don't understand. I need this job," I protested, trying to dig my feet into the ground, but the guy was stronger than he looked. "Hey, let go of me. That hurts."

The guide sneered. "You're going to hurt even more if you don't get out of here right this second."

I tried to protest again, but before I could get a word out, the Adonis from before appeared in the foyer. "Darren, what are you doing with our new maid?"

Darren? So, that's what this asshole's name was.

"I'll have the agency send a new one. This one is too clumsy." Darren sobered slightly and bowed his head before opening the door, no doubt to shove me out on my ass.

"Wait," the Adonis said. "I don't want a new maid. I want her." He pointed a long finger at me and made my heart lodge itself in my throat.

"But Master Wynn, I'm not sure that's a good idea." Darren pressed his lips into a thin line, clearly not happy with his employer.

And what was with the Master stuff? How old-fashioned and demeaning was that?

"Are you questioning me, Darren?" Master Wynn, or whatever this guy's name was, narrowed his eyes at the other man.

Darren let go of my arm and dropped to his knees. He shook his head profusely. "No, of course not, Master. I was just thinking of—" He cut himself off and pointed a finger toward the living room. "She broke the Qing vase!"

Wynn clucked his tongue. "That she did and now she is in our debt." A slow, wicked grin spread across his lips as he leered at me. "Unless you intend to pay us back for the vase?"

I shook my head, my mouth falling open.

"I didn't think so." Wynn offered me his hand, the other holding a bandage. "Now, let's get you wrapped up."

Glancing down at Darren, I hesitated. Then Darren's gaze met mine. There were anger and fear in those eyes, but also, there was a warning. Like he was trying to tell me something without Master Wynn knowing.

Either way, I didn't really have much of a choice. I needed this job. I'd already gotten fired from or quit so many jobs that the agency said this was my last chance. Even if these people ended up being sex-crazed freaks, it was better than living on the streets.

Master Wynn led me back to the living room and sat me down on the couch. He propped himself on the coffee table and took my hand gently in his, using a washcloth to clean off the blood. I watched his face as he worked on me. I hadn't noticed it before, but his eyes were dilated, and his nostrils flared. Did the sight of blood upset him?

Trying to make him feel more at ease, I withdrew my hand from his with a nervous laugh. "You know, I can do this myself. You're my boss, I can't really make you do this. I mean, I already owe you so much."

"Nonsense." Wynn flashed that wolfish grin once more. "What kind of employer would I be if I didn't take care of my employees?"

My eyes slid over to where Darren had been. The space was now empty, but the image of him on the ground before Wynn was burned into my mind. What kind of house had I gotten myself into?

Clearing my throat, I tried to make small talk. "So, the job description mentioned more than one tenant?"

"Ah, yes, my brothers." Wynn glanced up from wrapping my hand. "You'll meet them in good time." He paused for a moment and then continued working. "I noticed you didn't bring any bags with you? I thought we had told the agency we wanted a live-in maid."

"Oh, yeah. They told me. I only have one bag. It's in the car still." I shifted nervously in my seat.

I only had one bag because I had to sell most of what I owned to cover food and gas. They didn't need to know I've been living out of my car for the last few months, ever since I lost my full-time job to the economy and couldn't find a replacement.

Unfortunately, I hadn't been the savings type. So, my heart of gold landlord booted me the moment I couldn't pay rent. This in-home job should have been a godsend, but I was still holding on to my pride, what little left I had.

"Well, that's not a problem." Wynn taped the end of the bandage but didn't release my hand. His fingers stroked along the top of my hand making my pulse quicken. "I'm sure you will enjoy living here and if you need anything, an extra toothbrush, a shoulder to cry on, anything at all, just let me know." Wynn grinned and winked, making me forget all about the weird occurrence with Darren.

"Thank you, you don't know how much I need this job." I stopped and felt myself blush. "I mean, I know I owe you because of the vase, and I swear I'll pay you back, either with money or my time." I quickly spat out the words without knowing really what I was saying.

Wynn raised his hand, and I stopped talking. "I know, I know. How about we just worry about getting you settled in first and then we can deal with everything else?"

Nodding eagerly, I stood up when he did and followed him to the foyer. We paused by the door where Wynn pushed a button on an intercom.

A moment later, Darren's voice came over the speaker. "Yes, sir?"

"Please get Miss…" Wynn trailed off and looked to me. I mouthed, 'Billings,' and he nodded. "… Miss Billings' bag from the car."

"Yes, sir."

"And Darren?"

"Sir?"

"Make sure to clean up the mess in the living room."

"Of course, sir."

The warning in Wynn's voice was clear as well as the firm obedience from Darren. I wasn't exactly sure about the power dynamic in the house, but I knew Darren feared his boss. His yummy looks aside, Wynn hadn't been anything but nice to me since I entered the house. If I had been in Wynn's place and an employee had stepped over his bounds, I'd be pretty pissed too. The kneeling had been a bit much, but still, Darren had it coming.

Wynn turned back to me and held out his arm. "Shall we? I'll show you your room and then we can discuss your duties around here."

I stared down at his arm for a moment, the offer a bit old fashioned but nothing about this house had been normal so far. Shrugging a shoulder, I looped my arm through his, and he led me up the left staircase.

I tried my best to listen to him talk about the house, but the warmth of his body pressed against my side was distracting. I forced myself to watch his face to at least pretend to listen to him, but then I ended up staring at his lips. Those delicious pouty lips I wanted to bite.

"And this will be your room." Wynn opened a door down the hallway we had somehow ended up in. My eyes moved to the inside of the room, and I was surprised to see it was far nicer than I expected it.

A four-poster bed filled most of the room with a large dark green canopy above it. An expansive wardrobe stood to one side of the room as well as an antique desk that did not come from a flea market. To the right of the room was a door that was open, giving me a glance at the bathroom. There was a claw foot tub and even a vanity. It was far more than I deserved as the help.

"What do you think?" Wynn's voice in my ear startled me, and I spun around. Wynn had moved so much closer than before, putting us close enough to feel each other's breath.

"Uh," I stuttered and blinked rapidly, "it's great. Really wonderful. Bigger than my old apartment." I didn't know why I told him that. I wanted to keep my sad little existence to myself. No handouts for me.

However, Wynn acted as if he hadn't noticed my slip up. "Good, I would hate for you to be uncomfortable." His hand reached out and traced the curve of my jaw. Wynn's fingers burned along my flesh, and I ached to lean into his touch. He seemed to be studying me, searching for something. What that was, I didn't know.

All I knew was when his hand dropped, I instantly missed its warmth.

"I'll come to get you for dinner, and we can talk more then." Wynn nodded and then brushed past me.

My gaze followed him for a lot longer than it should have. Finally, when he was out of sight, I went into my room and collapsed on the bed. I was in so much trouble.

CHAPTER 3

Piper

I SPENT THE BETTER part of a half an hour just lying on the bed, wondering how I ended up in this situation. I had lived a good life. I went to work, paid my bills, and never bothered anyone. Then, one day, my job decided I wasn't worth it anymore.

Maybe because I hadn't done anything more than mediocre work. I had never strived to be the best. I did what I was asked and nothing extra. That was probably why they cut me loose and not any of the other employees.

My personal life wasn't much better. I had one or two friends who I talked to at least once a month. However, friends were exhausting, even more so when they weren't family. Family you could ignore, and they would always be there. Friends? Not so much.

My thoughts were interrupted by a knock on the door. Standing, I brushed my hands over my clothes. I hadn't worn anything spectacular to my first day. I was a maid, after all, I wouldn't want to dirty up anything nice. The slacks I wore were one of three pairs I owned. The other two were all that I had left of my work wardrobe from before, that and a few blouses and one pair of black heels. I had opted out of the black heels today and wore tennis shoes instead.

I grimaced down at my beat-up sneakers. They weren't really that impressive, especially for dinner in a place like this. There was another knock on the door just as I slipped into my heels. I raced for the door and pulled it open.

I expected to see Wynn since he had said he would come to get me, or at least Darren. However, the person waiting on the other side was neither of them. Not unless they had shrunk a few inches and colored their hair a bright red.

"Uh, hello." I held onto the door, prepared to shut it if the man in front of me meant ill will.

A sly grin slipped up the redhead's face, and the freckles across his nose popped out as he chuckled. The sound of it was like silk on my skin, and I shivered in pleasure. "Don't look so worried, sweetheart. I'm not going to eat you."

When he flashed his canines which like Wynn's were sharper than a normal person's. He must be one of the brothers. If that were the case, then I had no reason to fear him. I hoped.

"I'm Piper." I offered him a smile. "I'm the new maid."

The redhead rolled his eyes. "I know that, why do you think I'm here? Come on, they're waiting for us in the dining room." Unlike Wynn, he didn't offer me his arm to escort me to dinner. He pushed off the wall and tucked his hands into his pockets, sauntering down the hallway like he owned the place which I suppose he did.

I hurried after him. His legs weren't much longer than mine, so it wasn't that much of a feat. "So, you know my name. Am I going to get yours?"

The redhead's eyes slid over to me with a smirk. "Do you really need to know my name to clean the house?" He shook his head and let out a huff. "I don't even understand why

Wynn is allowing you to eat with us, but that's him." His eyes moved up and down my form, and I could see the twinkle in his eyes. "Always thinking with his dick."

I couldn't figure out if I should be offended or pleased. Knowing Wynn was attracted to me made something inside of me tingle. However, it was no secret that the guy beside me didn't much care for the hired help.

No love lost there.

My eyes trailed along the walls around me, taking in the antique furniture and large portraits. Much like the one in the living room, the paintings felt like they were watching me.

Please, God, don't let this house be haunted.

Sexy employers, I could do, even slightly weird ones. But ghosts? No, thank you. I was a wimp in the biggest sense of the word.

We turned a corner, and then we were at a different set of stairs than the ones from earlier. I was lucky I had someone here to guide me, or I'd be completely lost. The redhead didn't much seem to care if I ended up lost or not. He kept going as if I weren't even following him.

About halfway down the stairs, my foot caught on something, I was surprised it took this long, and my body propelled forward. Putting my hands out in front of me, the redhead's back came closer and closer to my face, and I hoped to God I didn't kill us both with my clumsiness.

However, before I could knock us both down the stairs, the guy spun around so fast I didn't register it until I was in his arms. My eyes squeezed shut, I inhaled his scent. He smelled of cinnamon and sandalwood, a smell that sunk low and settled in my core.

He growled.

My eyes shot open at the sound, my mouth parted at the heated look in his amber eyes. He had the same look about him that Wynn had when I had first met him in the living room. His tongue darted out and licked his lower lip, and for a moment, I thought he might close the distance between us. Then...

He dropped me.

"Oof," I groaned and rubbed my backside as I glared up at him. "What was that for?"

"Watch where you're going," he snapped, leaving me in the stairs by myself.

I gaped at the direction he had gone for a moment and then scrambled to my feet. Grumbling under my breath about rude ass rich boys, I rounded the stairs and slammed into his back. Once again, I was falling, but this time, I caught my hand on the railing before pulling myself back to my feet.

The redhead snickered.

Glaring daggers into his back, I followed him into a large dining room with an even bigger chandelier than the one in the foyer.

A long mahogany table big enough to sit twelve filled most of the room. Five of those spots were already taken, and surprisingly, Wynn was not at the head of the table.

A deep voice with a heavy European accent came from the man sitting at the head of the table. "Rayne, there you are." The man had long blonde hair and pale eyes that even from here were striking. When I stepped into the room from behind Rayne, the man frowned. "And you must be Miss Billings."

I didn't know why, but for some reason, I felt even less of a welcoming feeling from this man, clearly the leader of the brothers, than from Rayne or Darren. Unable to handle his stare, I folded my hands in front of me and ducked my head.

"Yes, thank you for having me in your home." I had the sudden urge to curtsy but didn't want to embarrass myself even further.

The man snorted. "You act as if you are a guest and not someone we hired. While I'm sure my brother, Wynn, has filled your head with all kinds of daydreams of your life here, I want to make sure you are clear in your duties."

I nodded. "I understand of course. I won't—"

"First rule. Do not speak unless I ask a question and then your answer should be straight to the point. No excuses and no long-winded stories." He glared at Wynn who pretended not to notice him. "Second, what happens in this house stays in this house, understood?"

I opened my mouth to answer him and then clamped it shut and simply nodded. It wasn't surprising they would want privacy. An NDA was usually required by most jobs. The fact that they hadn't made me sign one yet spoke volumes to their household. Either one of three things were happening.

One, the employees were so loyal to these men that they wouldn't dare say anything. One look around the room at the faces that had my panties wanting to evaporate right there made that answer pretty likely.

Or two, the other employees feared them which was just as likely from the way Darren had reacted to Wynn earlier and the way this one was putting off airs of a total tyrant.

And thirdly, the house could be total dullsville. Not likely with all this testosterone filling the room but it could happen. I bet they had revolving doors for their bedrooms.

I forced back a delightful shiver and made myself pay attention to the words he was saying. The man could read off a grocery list, and I'd orgasm, I swear.

The tyrant continued, not noticing my daydreaming, "Lastly, you will have a list of chores sent to your room each night for the following day. They are expected to be completed by the end of that day. Any that are not finished, you will have to add to your chores for the following day." The expression on his face told me he clearly expected me to finish each day's chores on that day.

Jesus, who shit in this guy's coffee? All fantasies I had about this guy just went down the toilet.

The man leaned back in his seat, his fingers placed into a steeple. "Now, I believe introductions should be made simply for convenience's sake. I don't expect you to socialize with any of us outside of what is expected for your work. Clear?"

Again, I nodded. This time, however, I was a bit more annoyed. This guy is really getting on my nerves.

"I, of course, am the eldest of the household. My name is Antoine Durand. You may call me Master Durand, but never just Antoine." His sharp tone made me want to flinch, but I curled my hands into fists, forcing myself not punch him in his stuck-up face.

"Here to my right is Marcus. He is the second oldest." Antoine pointed toward a large man with his hair buzzed down until there was only fuzz on top. He had a hard look to him that made me believe he wouldn't break the rules like Wynn.

"Next to Marcus is Wynn, which you have met already, the middle child." He rolled his eyes as Wynn grinned and winked at me.

It took everything in me not to blush and respond back in some way, but I had a feeling I would not earn any points with Antoine if I did. Master Durand. I reminded myself. Better get used to it now, so I didn't fuck up and call him by his name out loud.

Pointing a finger at the redhead next to me, Antoine scowled. "And Rayne you met already as well. He is the youngest." Continuing down the line, he pointed at a pair of twins on his left side. Both men had dark hair and a smile that made a dimple appear in their cheeks. "Draconius and Allister. They're the second youngest. Stay out of their way unless you want to be at the butt of their pranks."

The twins gave me matching sinister smirks that made my body react in an odd fashion. It was half fear and the other attraction? Not surprising since each brother was just as gorgeous than the last. I would think any female would have trouble not being attracted to them.

One of them, leaned forward on the table and growled, "Call me Drake."

Was it getting hot in here? I had the sudden urge to take a cold shower.

With all the introductions out of the way, Antoine stared at me expectantly. "Do you have any questions?"

I shook my head. "No." What I really wanted to ask was if he needed help taking that stick out of his ass, but I didn't want to get fired on my first day. I was lucky the vase incident hadn't got me booted out the door. The fact that Darren wasn't there just waiting for the word was unexpected.

As if listening to my thoughts, the tight-lipped butler appeared in the doorway on the other side of the room. "Dinner is ready."

Antoine inclined his head. "Very well. Darren, I expect you to show Miss Billings where she can eat her meals and teach her the rest of the house rules."

And with that, I was dismissed.

Darren didn't wait for me but marched back through the door he came. My eyes slid to the table in front of me, curiosity getting the best of me, but they didn't have any plates or silverware anywhere. Did they eat with their hands?

I didn't have long to stare at my new employers before Antoine locked that intense arrogant gaze back on me once more. "Did you need something else, Miss Billings?"

"No, no, sir. I mean, Master Durand." I stumbled over my words, irritated that there were even rules on how I was to address them.

Irritation covered Antoine's face, and he waved his hand at me. "Then get out."

Nodding again, I hurried after Darren, but Antoine's voice stopped me at the door. "And do try not to break anything else, Miss Billings."

Groaning, I realized I hadn't quite gotten off scot-free. I had a feeling this job was not going to be boring or easy. Lucky me.

CHAPTER 4

Antoine

I WATCHED THE SLIP of a girl walk, more like scurry, back into the kitchen. Tapping my finger against my lips, I hummed.

"Well, she's far more delicious than any of the other maids we've had," Draconius growled, his eyes lingering on the spot Piper Billings had been standing.

Leveling him with a stern glare, the side of my lip curls up in a snarl. "She is off limits."

"But—"

"Do not make me repeat myself." I picked up my wine glass and took a sip before sitting it back down. "We've gone through enough maids, we're lucky the agency sent us any others. They told us this would be the last one."

Wynn snorted, lounging like a lazy wild cat in his chair. "And you're surprised?"

Moving my attention to him, I narrowed my gaze. "Do not pretend like you were not partially responsible for at least half of those maids leaving."

"I said nothing of the sort." Wynn gave me a lopsided grin. "I'm just implying that we probably shouldn't be trying to keep human pets where there are no humans."

"I agree with, Wynn."

My eyes shot to Rayne who seemed far too annoyed at the maid already. "Using your gift, I see. What did you hear in that little head of hers?"

Rayne tousled his red hair and sniffed. "She's already half in love with Wynn. It's better to nip it in the bud before it bites us in the ass."

The vampire in question shifted a shoulder up. "I cannot help it if women are naturally attracted to me."

Glaring daggers at Wynn, Rayne growled, "They only want you because of your powers, not because you're such a catch, you self-absorbed snob."

Wynn didn't bother to rebuke Rayne's accusations, which he wouldn't. A narcissist like him only loved one person: himself.

I had to agree with Rayne on this one. For all his immaturity in age, he did have a point. If Miss Billings was already well on her way to being in love with Wynn, then we had a problem. God, what I wouldn't give for a nun right about now.

Except Wynn could charm the habit off even the most astute servant of God.

Coming to a decision, I lifted my glass in Wynn's direction. "Wynn, you are forbidden to use your powers on this new maid."

"Now hold on just a moment." Wynn finally sat up in his seat, a bit of worry on his face. Good, he should be worried. "Why do you think my powers have anything to do with it? I can get a girl without resorting to magic."

Draconius snorted. "Sure, you can."

Wynn lifted a brow. "Is that a wager I hear in your voice?"

Allister, Draconius's twin brother sighed and shook his head. "I think you rely far too much on your abilities to get a woman the old-fashioned way. It takes patience, something you lack greatly."

"I have a far greater chance than you." Wynn pointed a finger at Allister. "You with your smooth-talking ways. You are crippled by that silver tongue of yours. There's no way you could get into a woman's pants or heart without speaking."

I stifled a groan. Once these idiots set their minds on something it was hard pressed to get them to change it.

"You want to bet?" Allister sneered.

Rayne slammed his hand on the table as he stood. "I thought the point of this meeting was to agree that we weren't going to mess with the new maid, and here you three are, making bets on who could get into her pants the fastest without using your powers."

Tired of listening to them squabble, I met Rayne's gaze. "Too true. Thank you, Rayne." Glancing around the table, I made sure they were all paying attention to me before I continued. "No one at this table will be trying to do anything with Miss Billings. If you want a woman, do it out of the house. I will not have this household go to shambles because you cannot keep it in your pants."

Rayne sat back down and sighed. "Why can't we just hire a cleaning service? They come in, clean, and leave. Why have a maid live on site at all?"

Giving Rayne a measured gaze, I tossed my hair over my shoulder. "Because we cannot have some outsider snooping around where their noses don't belong. Eventually, we will gain Miss Billings' trust and then we won't have to tip toe around in our own home."

Rayne let out a rude sound. "Fat chance that's gonna happen. These three can't stop thinking with their dicks long enough to get her to trust us."

"That is why you will keep tabs on her." I locked eyes with him, pushing my will into my words. "I want to know what she's thinking at all times. If she finds out what we are and decides to run, I want to know."

Inclining his head like the good, obedient brother, Rayne stood again and left us either to get his own meal or brood.

I wasn't fooled. I knew Rayne hated his ability to see into the minds of humans, especially ones he cared about. If he was smart, he would keep his emotions close to the chest and not let them get in the way of what had to be done. I was tired of having to break someone new in. We had Darren, but there were simply too many of us for him to handle us and this big house.

"He's going to hate you for this," Wynn murmured, his eyes coming up off the table. "You know how he fee—"

"I know," I intoned seriously.

Marcus, who hadn't said a word during the whole exchange, shifted at my right. "It's necessary."

Wynn glared at the mountain of a man. "To who?"

"If you want Rayne to stop being an immature brat, then you need to stop treating him like a child," I simply stated, turning my head as the front door opened.

I could hear Darren greet the guests as they came in. I could smell the heavy perfume of the donors before they even hit the dining room. Several women entered the room, each of them in skin-baring clothing. If anyone on the outside saw them, they would think they might be prostitutes, which they were in a way. They sold their bodies, yes, but not for sex.

No, sex was far easier to pay for than what we wanted, what we needed.

"Now this is more like it." Draconius leered, licking his lips like a wolf about to devour his meal. He stood from the table and came up beside a voluptuous brunette. Slipping a hand behind her head, he tilted her head back. "Are you scared, my lovely?"

The woman gave Draconius a sultry smile. "Do you want me to be?"

I didn't pay much more attention to him or my other brothers as they each picked their donor. In most households, the head of the house would pick first, but I'd never been one to care. Blood was blood, no matter the source. However, when the petite blonde came my way, I frowned. She reminded me far too much of the maid we had just been discussing.

Wearing a low-cut, revealing dress, she sauntered over to my side. Her fingers played along her neck line as her eyes devoured me. "Where would you like me, master?"

That one word made my groin harden, pressing up against the fabric of my slacks. I had control issues. I knew it. The others knew it. It was no doubt the reason I had the power to make someone do as I wanted, even against their will. I'd always been this way, even in life some hundred years ago. Now, even in my undead life, I craved it.

"Here," I purred, moving back from the table so she could slide into my lap. Her arms wrapped around my shoulders, and she leaned in as if to kiss me. Not giving her the chance, I tangled my fingers in her hair and pulled her head to the side.

She gasped with a mixture of pain and pleasure. I could already smell her arousal and I'd barely touched her. Those who took this job weren't in it just for the pay, though it was astronomical compared to paying for sexual favors. They wanted this every bit as much as we did.

I lifted my head briefly to see the others had already begun to feed. Wynn used his powers at the same time, causing the woman to orgasm while he tasted her. I would never bring someone to orgasm with just my touch. I could only command them to enjoy it, and they would. However, with this one, I thought as I adjusted my hold on the blonde, she would love it no matter what.

Without warning, I plunged my fangs into her neck and drank deeply. She cried out, her little hands gripping my shirt and no doubt wrinkling the fabric. I forced myself to stop thinking and to focus on the beat of her heart.

Thudump. Thudump. Thudump.

Though the woman in my arms was perfectly good and the blood sweeter than most I'd tasted, I couldn't help but think of Miss Billings. Those big brown eyes and soft mouth. Her immediate arousal as she took in each and every one of us. Would our little maid's heart beat quicken at my touch? Despite my warnings to my brothers, I couldn't help but want to find out.

CHAPTER 5

Piper

THE DOOR DARREN HAD gone through led to the kitchen. Not just any kitchen though, it was one of those T.V. kitchens most of us peasants only dreamed of. It had a double top stove with a large range overhead, and the island and counters were all covered in a dark marble that I would fear I'd scratch if I touched it.

Uh, oh. Put away the china.

"Finally," Darren sniffed, not any happier for me to be there than I was. "You may eat your meals in here at the bar or in your room. Nowhere else."

I slid onto one of the barstools and nodded curtly, not trusting myself to be civil.

Darren went about taking a plate from the cabinet and filling it with some kind of beef and vegetable concoction on the stove. Whatever it was smelled heavenly. At this point, I'd have taken anything other than fast food. I was surprised I hadn't gotten as big as a house from of all the crap I ate because of my prior living conditions.

"I'm sure Master Durand has already made it clear, but you are here for one thing, to do your job, not to socialize and not to poke your nose into the masters' business." He placed the plate in front of me along with a glass of lemonade, his brown eyes narrowing to slits. "Some days, you might finish your chores early. If this happens, you have the rest of the day to yourself. You will get Sundays off for you to take care of any personal things."

"Oh, wow. A full day off to myself." The words slipped from my mouth before I could stop them. I paused for a moment, expecting to be chastised for my slip up, but Darren had better manners than me and simply huffed, pressing his lips together until they thinned into a fine line.

Not pushing my luck, I turned my attention back to my plate. I picked up my fork and took a bite of my meal, pretending to listen to him once more. I couldn't help but let out a hum of pleasure at the taste. This was absolutely divine.

God, I haven't had food like this in forever.

"So happy you enjoy my food."

My eyes snapped open and flushed as I realized Darren was staring at me with a bemused look on his face. It was as close to a smile I had ever seen on him. I tucked that little tidbit into the back of my mind for later.

"Are you and me the only people who work here? I haven't seen any other employees." I waved my fork around in the air at the obvious lack of workers. "Seems a bit odd for such a big house."

Darren made a plate for himself as he spoke. "I handle the household, as in I answer the phones, the door, and anything else the masters need. I also, on occasion, cook as well." He tilted his head toward my plate of food.

I felt like he was telling me not to get used to it. Oh, well. The cook couldn't be worse than some of the questionable gas station food I'd eaten.

Never eat sushi from a guy named Lenny at the corner mart. Your intestines will hate you for the whole weekend.

"The regular cook is Miss Gretchen," Darren continued. "She only comes a few times a week. Miss Gretchen also makes some premade meals and places them in the fridge." He gestured toward the large double door refrigerator before coming over to sit by me.

"And I clean the house?" I arched a brow, finding it kind of hard to believe that this massive house ran on only three people.

Darren seemed to understand my reservation. "The masters keep to themselves for the most part and are remarkably tidy. You shouldn't have too much trouble keeping up with your chores. Just remember the rules, and you will be fine."

Arching a doubtful brow at him, I shook my head. "You obviously don't know me very well. Rules? Fine, but believe it or not, I attract trouble like flies on shit." I bit my lower lip and flushed. "Pardon my language. I just thought I'd forewarn you."

Darren gave a resigned sigh. "As much as I appreciate the gesture, I have to warn you as well. Any trouble you may cause will not end well for you, and I don't mean from the unemployment agency."

I nodded in understanding at his wilting glare.

Stay out of trouble. Boy, have I got my work cut out for me.

We both ate our meals in silence after that. I could hear the murmurs of the masters from the dining rooms, but they were too low for me to make out what they were saying. I hadn't seen Darren take them food, so I wasn't sure exactly what they were eating.

After several minutes, I worked up the courage to ask. "If we're eating this, what are the masters eating?" The word 'masters' felt weird on my tongue as if I should be wearing a collar and holding a whip.

Darren gave me an evasive look. "The masters are on a special diet. You wouldn't find it very appealing."

Probably one of those fake gluten-free diets. I grimaced, the masters losing several hotness points because of it.

When I finished my meal, I took it to the sink and rinsed it before sticking it in the dishwasher, something I had been taught to do since I was young. I turned around to see Darren watching me with a curious expression.

"What? I know how to wash a dish." I shrugged and started back toward the dining room, but Darren stopped me.

"Don't go that way." I glanced back at him, my brow furrowed. "The staircase over there will take you back upstairs and comes out near your room. Use this one from now on when coming in and out of the kitchen. The dining room is reserved for the masters alone."

Wrinkling my nose, I wiped my hands against each other and changed my direction to head for the stairs. However, once more, I was stopped by Darren's voice.

"By the way, if you are in your room, you should always lock your door, especially at night." He gave me one of those firm, no-nonsense looks that didn't leave any room for questioning.

So, I didn't.

Taking the stairs two at a time, I couldn't wait to get to my room and process all of this. Today had been an interesting day, to say the least, and I could only assume it would only get worse.

When I got to my room, I worked on unpacking what little I had and made a note to myself to go buy some more suitable work clothes. I couldn't imagine cleaning in dress pants, and they hadn't specified a dress code. By the time it was time for bed, I had showered and changed into an oversized t-shirt. I pulled back the covers of my new bed and sighed into the sheets.

Even the thread counts of the servant's beds were better than anything I had before. It was like sleeping on a cloud.

I'd barely closed my eyes when there was a knock on my door. I sat up, but the doorknob turned before I could answer, and I cursed myself for not locking it.

A dark head poked in the doorway and when those piercing blue eyes saw that I wasn't asleep, Wynn threw the door open. "Ah, you're still awake."

I scooched up in the bed, pulling my covers closer to me. "Uh, yeah. Was just about to go to bed actually."

Wynn hummed, and his eyes went around my room. "The last few maids didn't do much to this room. They didn't last long enough." He winked at me. "But I have a feeling you'll be different."

Clearing my throat and yelling at my libido to chill the fuck out, I wrung my hands in my lap. "I hope you're right."

We're quiet for a moment, and I wondered what the gorgeous man was doing in my room. It certainly broke the no fraternizing rule his brother had all but drilled into my head.

"So, your brothers seem nice." I figured I'd at least prod him for answers since we were breaking the rules and everything.

Wynn's eyes crinkled at the sides. "Then you don't know them very well."

"Not as nice as you?" I teased.

Snorting, Wynn moved over to my bed, his fingertips trailing along the line of my legs under the bedspread before sitting down at my side. "Let's just say they lack my charms as well as several other redeeming qualities."

"Oh. Well, I'm sure we'll get along just fine." I gave him a hopeful smile.

"Enough about my brothers," Wynn said, taking my injured hand in his own. "Tell me about you. Do you have any family?"

My brows scrunched together as he unwrapped my hand, his fingers brushing along my skin and making me shudder. "Uh, yeah." I licked my lips and tried not to faint. "I have parents and siblings. We don't really talk."

"That's too bad." His voice was low, his eyes intently focused on the cut on my hand. It had stopped bleeding already but still stung. "Does it hurt?"

"A little."

"Here, I'll fix that." Wynn leaned forward and brushed his lips against the palm of my hand. I felt the touch of his lips all the way down to my toes. I curled my legs close to me, hoping he couldn't tell how turned on I was by him.

He peered up at me from beneath his long lashes, his nostrils flaring. "Better?"

Swallowing hard, I jerked my head up and down twice and breathed out, "Yes."

Even with my reassurance, he didn't release my hand. Wynn's mouth hovered over my skin. My pulse jerked at the heat of his breath as he laid a kiss on my wrist. I squirmed in place, the tiny panties I wore becoming increasingly uncomfortable.

"Wynn."

Antoine's voice startled both of us. I jerked my arm out of Wynn's grasp and shoved it under the covers as if that would save me from the hot, needy feeling swirling around in between my thighs. I couldn't look up at my boss my face, hot and stinging from embarrassment.

Wynn didn't seem to have the same issue. He flashed me a toothy grin before standing. Strolling across the room, he gave me a languid wave. "Good night, little maid."

I didn't reply, keeping my eyes down on my duvet. However, when the bedroom door didn't shut right away, I chanced a look up.

Antoine's pale eyes bore into me, making me squirm for a completely different reason. I opened my mouth to explain what had happened, but Antoine didn't give me the chance.

"Lock your door. I won't be responsible for what happens next time if you don't."

I bobbed my head so fast my eyes rolled in my head.

"Good night, Miss Billings."

"Good night, Master Durand." The door clipped shut before I could finish my sentence.

Jerk.

These guys were going to be the death of me if they didn't fire me first. Sinking into my sheets once more, I started to close my eyes before Wynn's face flashed in my head, hungry and leering. I ran my fingers over where he had kissed me.

Dropping my hand, I sighed. Stop daydreaming, Piper. You have a job to do, and that didn't include banging the bosses. I had my battery-operated friend for that.

Jumping out of the bed, I raced across the room and turned the lock. I hurried back to my bed and dove beneath the covers. Snuggling down, I reached over and flicked the lamp switch. Letting out a small moan of pleasure, I realized something.

No guy, no matter how sexy, was worth giving up this thread count. I chuckled to myself as I drifted off to sleep.

That night, I dreamed of my new employers as dark figures surrounding me, taunting me, and demanding me to come with them. Wynn was the most eager of the six brothers to have me join them. By the time I woke the next morning, I had tossed and turned myself so much that my sheets were tangled around my body.

I fought against my confines and ended up on the floor with a thud. Groaning, I grabbed my head and rubbed my eyes. The light pierced through the shades and blinded me as I cracked open my eyes. I had forgotten to close them the night before. Why this one room had the curtains open and the rest of the house didn't, I would never know.

Glancing over at the alarm clock, it read just after seven, about the time I usually woke for work. Guess some habits were hard to break.

Standing, I moved across the cold wooden floor to the bathroom to shower and begin the day. Halfway across the room, I noticed a slip of paper just inside the door. Cocking my head to the side, I went over and picked it up.

On the paper was a simple list. No greeting. No thank you. Just a list of chores.

1. Gather the laundry.
2. Start laundry.
3. Vacuum the living room.
4. Clean windows on second-floor servants wing.
5. Switch laundry in between jobs.
6. Fold and return to correct room.

Man, they hadn't been kidding when they said I *might* have time off in the evening. From this list, I'd be lucky to be able to take a piss or a lunch break without being behind.

Sighing, I threw the list on the side table and gathered my clothes. After seeing the list, I couldn't very well take a long shower like I had planned. Instead, I quickly washed and then got distracted beneath the shower pressure.

God, forget the thread count. No guy was worth giving up this shower pressure. My muscles sang with delight as the water beat down on my shoulders.

Before I knew what I was doing, my mind had conjured up Wynn from last night, his mouth on my hand and then moving to my wrist. In my mind, he didn't stop there. Those pouty lips found the bend of my elbow and then finally after several moments of teasing my mouth. My fingers stroked in long needy movements along my skin, cupping my breasts and plucking at my nipples. My other hand dipped between my legs, and my knees almost buckled at my touch.

"Fuck." I gasped, having never been so turned on in my life. It didn't take more than a few flicks of my clit before I was bent over, gasping for breath.

My eyes fluttered open, and I stared hard at the side of the tub. Shaking my head to clear the post orgasm haze from my head, I climbed out of the tub and quickly dried off. I didn't give myself time to think much about what I'd just done as I went about brushing my teeth and hair. I pulled my long blonde hair up into a bun and lightly applied some mascara and lip gloss. I didn't know why I was bothering, but for some reason, being in a house full of attractive men made me want to look my best. I took a moment to stare at my light brown eyes. Even now they shone like someone who'd just been thoroughly fucked.

"Pfft." I tossed my head from side to side and turned from the mirror.

Since they hadn't given me a dress code, I went for jeans and a pale green t-shirt. I slipped my tennis shoes back on and grabbed the list before heading for the door. Glancing one way and then the other, I noticed the hallway was completely empty.

Were my employers even up yet? I huffed and rolled my eyes. Probably not. They probably didn't know the meaning of the word morning.

Snorting at the lives of the rich, I found the staircase that I had come up the night before and headed down it. The smell of eggs and bacon filled my nose before I reached the bottom, and I found a plump older woman working at the stove.

Thank God, another woman. I thought I was going to drown in all the testosterone around here.

"Hello," I greeted the woman, already feeling hopeful for the day. "You must be Miss Gretchen. I'm Piper."

Gretchen turned from the stove with a bright smile. "You got that right." She pointed the spatula in her hand at the bar. "Have a seat, I'll have breakfast ready in a moment."

Taking a seat, I grabbed the pot of coffee off the counter and poured some into the cup in front of me. Searching around for creamer, I moved over to the fridge.

"Creamer is in the door, bottom shelf," Miss Gretchen helpfully supplied.

I found the creamer and poured a heaping amount into my cup. Sipping deeply from the cup, I sighed. Just what I needed to start the day.

"Oh, dear. If you're already that dejected, I don't have high hopes for you to get through the week." Miss Gretchen tsked as she sat a plate before me. The scent of it made my stomach rumble in pleasure.

"I know," I breathed, placing my elbow on the counter and leaning my face on my palm. "It's just so different than what I'm used to." As I finished my explanation, I scooped a forkful of eggs into my mouth. Suddenly, I was starving and inhaled my food like it was the last thing I'd ever eat.

"Well, I'm glad you have an appetite on you at least. These young masters barely touch anything I make." Gretchen shook her head, one hand on her hip. "I don't even see the reason for me being here half the time, but with you here, at least I'll feel a bit more useful."

"Well, my mother did always say I was a bottomless pit. She wasn't sure where I put it all." I patted my flat stomach and shrugged a shoulder. "Fast metabolism, I guess." I grinned at her as I finished my plate and picked up my coffee cup. Just as I wondered how to go about asking how long Gretchen had worked there, Darren showed up in the kitchen doorway.

"Are you finished? I'm supposed to show you where the laundry room is." He didn't wait for me to answer but disappeared back through the doorway he had specifically told me not to go through.

Glancing at Gretchen, she nodded her head. "Go on ahead. I'll take care of these." She took my plate and cup and took them to the sink.

"Thank you and for the meal as well." I wiped my mouth and quickly followed Darren. It was barely eight, and already they had me on my toes. The end of the day couldn't come soon enough.

CHAPTER 6

Piper

I COULD SAY ONE thing about Darren. He was efficient. He showed me the laundry room and where each of the masters kept their baskets for when I collected them.

Collecting them was a different matter.

I had no idea whose room was whose. I needed a map or labeling system. Unfortunately, I didn't think that Darren was going to draw me a map.

Thankfully, I didn't need one. The hallway Darren pointed me to, the one to the right side of the stairs from the front of the house, had a row of rooms that were in the order of the masters' ages.

The first door on the left was Antoine's, which I definitely didn't want to go into. I didn't think any of them would be awake by now and really didn't want to go waking up my new bosses. However, it was on my to-do list. It wasn't like I had a choice.

Darren didn't offer me any tips for how to go about getting the laundry from the rooms, so I was on my own against six handsome strangers, two of which I knew didn't like me. One of them wanted in my pants. And, well, the other three? I didn't really know anything about them except they were large and Antoine's warning about the twin tricksters.

Sighing, I decided to start with the last door, Rayne's room. I knocked on the door, but there was no answer. I waited a moment and then knocked again. Still no answer.

Slowly, I turned the doorknob and pushed the door open. The room was dark, and no sign of life could be seen from where I stood. Inching inside, I glanced toward the bed. Empty.

Of all the brothers I sure as hell didn't expect the youngest, who looked like he was barely twenty, would be up at the time of day. Man, I remembered what it was like to be that young. Okay, hold up. It was only a few years ago, okay, seven, but it's not like it was that long ago. However, while I was in college, I didn't get up before noon unless I absolutely had too. Even then, I made excuse after excuse to make my classes in the afternoon.

Sadly, sleep was one thing I had to give up when I ended up living in my car. It's hard to sleep when anyone could come by and see me sleeping. I'd been woken up by a cop or two already for being parked in a no parking zone for too long, not to mention the one time I woke up to a homeless man jerking off in front of my window.

I shuddered at the thought.

Not wanting to come face to face with the man himself, I hurried into the room and found his laundry basket. Of course, it stunk to high heaven. Full of basketball socks and wet towels, no doubt.

I dumped his basket into my bag and realized that one bag was not going to cut it. Groaning, I lugged the bag over my shoulder and sat it outside the door. So glad I chose to wear jeans and a t-shirt for this. I was not going to waste my good work clothes for lugging laundry around, especially, laundry that smelled like something had crawled up in it and died.

Pulling out another bag from the pile that Darren had given me, I went to the next room.

If memory served, it would be one of the twins. No idea which one it belonged to though since there were no names on the rooms. I knocked on their door just like I did Rayne's and once more came up with no answer.

Shoving the door open, I wasted no time crossing the room and finding the laundry basket. Whichever's room this was, at least they didn't stink as bad as Rayne's. Darren hadn't been kidding about them being tidy though. Not a single sock or pair of jock shorts on the floor. Amused by the concept of a neat man, I dumped the basket into the bag. When done, I started for the door but paused at a side table where some mail sat.

Figuring I could use that to figure out which twin's room it was, I picked up the first envelope I found. The front of it said it was from some company called Opos Bank. Shrugging it off as some odd named bank, I glanced down at the name.

Allister Durand.

This was Allister's room. I tapped the envelope on my hand and glanced around the room with a nod.

Good to know.

I returned the envelope to the side table and continued on my way. I went through the rest of the rooms, each one as empty as the last. I wasn't sure if I was happy or disappointed about that. A small part of me hoped I'd at least catch one of them in their boxers or even coming out of the shower.

I drooled a bit as an image of a wet and naked Wynn came to mind. The tiny towel he was wearing in my mind barely covered anything, and he had a teasing grin on his face as he 'accidentally' dropped it.

"You seem to be doing alright." The very voice of the man I was daydreaming about appeared before me. "And here I thought I'd check to make sure the locals hadn't run you off yet."

My face heated, and I ducked my head. "No, I'm alright. Actually, you're the first I've seen other than Darren or Gretchen that is." I gathered the bags up and started to lug them back toward the stairs. Man, this was harder than it looked.

"Want some help with that?" Wynn tried to help me pick up the bags, but I waved him off.

"No, I got it. It's my job after all."

Wynn laughed that delicious laugh of his, and I almost melted right there. "That may be, but you are clearly struggling. I'm just doing the gentlemanly thing by offering to help."

Smiling despite myself, I let go of the bags and turned to him. "I suppose I could let you carry one."

"Oh?" Wynn arched a brow and moved in closer, reaching out to take the bag. Our hands brushed against each other, and my breath caught.

After I reminded myself how to breathe, I licked my lips and offered him a weak smile. "Well, we can't have it being said that you weren't a gentleman, now can we?"

"No, I suppose not." Wynn leaned toward me, and I was frozen to the spot. His piercing blue eyes locked with mine, his pupils dilating as his nostrils flared. My eyes started to flutter shut, but all of a sudden, Wynn backed away. "Your hand is bleeding again."

My brows furrowed at his random statement. Glancing down at my injured hand, I could see the red bleeding through the bandage I had replaced after my shower this morning.

"Oh, I guess I am. Probably aggravated it with all the bag moving," I murmured out loud. When I glanced up from my hand, Wynn was gone.

Staring at the place he had once stood, I wondered what his problem was. He had been nice enough to bandage my hand yesterday, but clearly, I had been right about him being queasy about blood. Although, that didn't stop him from feeling up my hand and wrist last night.

Snorting, I shook my head. Strange men.

With Wynn gone, I had to take all the bags back downstairs myself, which ended up taking half the morning. By the time I was done, I stank worse than Rayne's laundry.

My stomach growled, ready to eat itself, and I wasn't even half done with my chores.

I think I'd earned a break. At least, a snack. You know, to keep my strength up.

Gretchen wasn't in the kitchen, nor Darren when I arrived. However, there was a sandwich sitting in the middle of the island with my name on a sticky note stuck to the edge of the plate. Pulling the plate over to the edge of the counter, I sat down with a sigh.

With no one there to bother me, I took my sweet time eating my sandwich and then putting my plate in the dishwasher. Feeling parched after my sandwich, I opened the fridge and pulled out a bottle of water. Twisting the cap open, I chugged the cool liquid and waited for the clothes to buzz.

What would it be like to live in this house for real? Instead of me doing the laundry and cleaning, I'd be a lady of luxury. No need to work because I'd have millions I'd inherited from my parents. I tried to imagine what kind of parents the masters had. They were each so different it was hard to figure out if they had the same parents or if they were brothers by choice.

All I could say was they had good taste in siblings.

I giggled to myself and tossed my bottle in the trash as the clothes buzzed. I switched the clothes from the washer to the dryer and then headed toward the living room to work on the next item on my list.

It was strange. As I went through one chore after the other, besides the one appearance of Wynn, I didn't run into any of the other brothers. Darren was the only one I saw, and usually, that was only for him to bark more orders at me or complain I wasn't doing something right. It wasn't until the sun had set and I was dead on my feet that I ran into one of the masters.

"Ah, so you're still here." Rayne appeared in the kitchen and opened the fridge. He pulled out a bottle with his name on the label and took a deep drink. There's a bottle in there for each of them, but I wasn't sure what exactly it was. I just assumed some kind of protein drink.

I watched as the bottle came down from Rayne's mouth that his lips were stained red. Definitely some kind of health drink. I wanted to gag just thinking about it. No, thank you. I'd take my vegetables the all-natural way, not smashed or juiced to a pulp.

"Did you think I wouldn't?" I asked, digging my fork into the left-over container Gretchen had set out for me.

Rayne snorted. "We have a bet going actually."

"A bet?" I choked on the drink I had just taken a gulp of. "Really?"

Beaming at me, Rayne nodded. "Yep. I bet you wouldn't last a day."

Rolling my eyes, I turned back to my food. "Well, you lost. I'm still here."

"Not for long. Night's fallen." Rayne flashed his canines at me and walked out the door with his bottle in hand.

"Well, that was cryptic," I muttered to myself and finished my meal. After I was done, I gathered up the laundry that had finished, preparing to take them back to their owner's rooms before going to my room for the night.

Taking the clothes back was going to be harder than picking them up, since my chances of running into one of my new employers was high. Thankfully, Rayne was doing whatever college level douche bags did so I could easily drop his clothes off without a problem. The same went for Allister's clothes. However, when I went to drop Drake's clothing off, I wasn't so lucky.

"Why hello there. Miss Billings, is it? Or can I call you Piper?" Drake grinned at me, his body only partly covered in a towel, his skin still wet from his shower. It was like he had read my mind and knew about my daydream earlier today, and as my eyes followed the trail of water moving down Drake's rippling abs and to the bulge below the terry cloth, I knew I was in trouble.

Astronomically.

CHAPTER 7

Piper

MY BRAIN SHORT-CIRCUITED. I didn't know what to do. Should I leave or continue with my work? Honestly, I was having a hard time just getting my brain to function. My eyes trailed down Drake's body, taking in the black tattoo of some kind of bird on his chest before once more landing on the obvious tent in the towel. I swallowed. Such a hard time.

"Are you going to stand there all day or give me my clothes?" Drake smirked and held his hand out. "I don't really have anything else to wear. Unless... you prefer the towel?"

No. I preferred nothing at all, but I wasn't going to tell him that.

"No, no. I'm sorry, you just caught me off guard." I shook my head from side to side, making my ponytail hit my shoulders, and hustled further inside to set the bag down. I tried to hurry back to the door, but Drake's gravelly voice stopped me.

"So, you don't like the towel?" Drake said in such a strange way that I had to pause and look back at him, just in time to see him drop the towel on the ground. Against my will, my eyes instantly locked onto what had been hidden beneath, and my mouth grew dry. "Ah, I see you like me better this way, huh?"

I couldn't find my words. What were words? Thoughts? Thick muscular thighs. His cock hung long, hard, and perfect between his legs, and it was coming even closer to me.

Jerking my eyes away from Drake's perfect equipment, I felt my face heat considerably. Backing up, I held my hands up in front of me as if that would ward off what I'd just seen. Even a priest couldn't exorcize that image from my head, not that I would want him to. My vibrator and I would relish in this memory later, when it was dark, and no one could hear me scream.

"I'm so sorry. I'll just go now." I hated the words even as they came out of my mouth, but if this wasn't fraternizing, I didn't know what was. Antoine had already gotten onto me once, and if you counted the vase breaking when I got here, that was already two strikes against me. I didn't want to find out what happened when I got to three.

"Why the rush?" Drake asked, closing in on me until my back hit the door. "You just got here. We haven't gotten the chance to get to know each other yet, and I so want you to feel comfortable here in our home. Don't you?"

His breath felt hot against my face, and I turned my head to the side. Just standing there with a gorgeous, naked man was playing havoc on my body. Now he had to get up close and personal. I wasn't sure I'd be able to keep my hands, let alone my mind, to myself.

"Tell me, Piper," Drake growled, his nose brushing along the curve of my neck, the pulse there beating a mile a minute. "Have you ever been had by a man?"

"W-what?" I gawked at him, shifting away from him as much as I could with the door at my back. The feral look in his eyes scared me and turned me on all at the same time. What the hell was wrong with me?

Drake didn't seem to have the same thoughts as me and brushed a hand over my hair before grabbing my ponytail, tugging it just enough to make my head bend back to meet his hungry gaze.

"You know what I mean. Have you ever..." His other hand moved down along the outside of my thigh, causing them to press together. "... let a man into your glorious haven?"

I snorted. I couldn't help it. Glorious haven? Come on now. How cliché was that?

"What?" Drake jerked back from me, a look of confusion making his beautiful face even more attractive.

Shaking my head, I slipped out of his grasp. "Your brother was right about you. You really know how to pull a prank." Grabbing the door handle, I pulled it open, but it was slammed shut by Drake's hand.

Startled, I spun around to give him a piece of my mind. Playing with my mind was one thing, but he was pushing the joke too far.

"I'm not joking." Drake bared his teeth at me before caging me in between his arms once more. "You should not have come here, little girl. Your type tends to get eaten up by mine, especially if you smell like that." He took a big whiff of me, and a low rumbling escaped from his chest.

Frowning at his manhandling, I shoved at his chest. "Now, you listen to me here. You might think you are the hot shit which, well, you are." I let my eyes drift down for a moment before catching myself and poking my finger at his chest. "But I'm not some piece of ass you can mess with. I need this job, and I'm not going to do anything that might jeopardize it. That includes getting wrapped up in the likes of you."

Drake stared down at me for a moment as if he couldn't quite believe I had told him off. Then he threw his head back and laughed, a sound that I hated to love so much. "Oh, you poor, sweet thing. You think your words will save you?"

"Well, I–"

"If your job is what you are worried about, I wouldn't worry too much about it." Drake cupped my face in his hand, stroking his thumb across my lower lip. "Antoine is not the only voice in this house. If I want you to stay, you will stay."

I found myself frozen to the spot. The dark pools of his brown eyes were so entrancing that I couldn't look away from them. I was at his mercy, and there was nothing I could do. Part of me started to panic, my breathing coming in as quick gasping breaths and my heart thumping against my ribs. My reaction only made Drake smile wider as if he enjoyed my displeasure.

"Now, stay still while I get a taste of you." Drake leaned down, his mouth opening wide.

I wasn't sure exactly what he was going to do. Give me a hickey? Was he one of those people who liked to lick? I could get down with that if it weren't on my neck. Or my ear. God, people who liked someone sticking their tongue in their ear were just weird.

Oh. My thoughts went quiet at the first touch of his tongue. *Oh, my.*

The warm wet muscle slid along the line of my neck just as the door behind me burst open. Thrown from the door, I fell to the ground, whatever spell I was under broken. Drake still stood on his feet but was now a few feet away, and his shorts had magically appeared on his form.

"What do you want, Marcus?" Drake asked his older brother calmly as if he hadn't had his hands and mouth on me.

Marcus glanced to where I now sat on the ground and then back to Drake who had a smug grin on his face. "You know the rules."

"And I didn't break them." Drake held his hands up in front of him. "No harm, no foul. She's fine." He turned those eyes on me and waved a hand. "Tell him. I didn't do anything to you."

I crawled to my feet, my legs a bit wobbly beneath me. Clearing my throat, I glared at Drake. "You're such an ass," I shouted before I marched out of the room and back into the hallway, not waiting to see what they said.

I should have been panicking for calling my boss, well, one of my bosses, an ass, but he'd started it. He'd flashed me and then proceeded to molest me. Okay, so it wasn't like I didn't enjoy it but still.

Ugh. Fucking men.

Hushed voices followed me as I moved away from Drake's door and to his brother Allister's. I held my breath and hoped that he wasn't in there as well. If one twin was like that, then the other probably was as well.

Thankfully, Allister was in his bathroom when I entered. I dropped his bag off and darted out of the room before I caught him with his pants down as well. I finished handing out the other bags to Wynn and Marcus, the latter probably still reaming into Drake about breaking the rules.

Fucking deserved it too.

Finally, all I had left was Antoine's, the one I was least excited to deliver.

I paused outside of his door, contemplating leaving the bag on the floor and making for my room. Come on, Piper. He's just a man. If you can't handle being in the same room as them, then you can't do this job. And we need this job.

Mustering up all my courage, I knocked on the door. The sound so much louder than I expected it to be and I waited for no more than a second before a voice from inside answered.

"Enter."

With my nerves already on edge, I slowly opened the door. Antoine stood by his window, looking at some papers. The drapes were pulled back for once so that the night sky could be seen. It was a beautiful sight but paled in comparison to the man before me.

Someone shouldn't look so good in just slacks and a white button-down shirt. His long blonde hair was braided down his back, and his pale eyes intensely stared at the papers in his hands. He didn't even look up from them when I entered the room.

"I have your laundry." I held the bag up lamely.

"Put it over there." Antoine gestured his hand flippantly to the dresser.

Nodding, I moved over to the large dresser and sat the bag down. I was surprised they hadn't asked me to fold and put up their clothes as well, but as Darren had informed me, they were each particular about their things and didn't want me snooping.

Ha! Me? Snoop? I didn't care a flip about these bastards. I just wanted to do my job and get paid. Maybe once I saved enough, I could get a different job and my own apartment.

One could dream.

I made my way back to the door but stopped, my eyes going back to Antoine who hadn't moved or looked up from his papers. Should I say goodnight? He had told me not to speak unless spoken to which I had already messed up when I entered his room. So, I couldn't very well get in any more trouble by being polite. Right?

"Good night, Master Durand." The words had barely left my mouth before Antoine called out to me.

"Miss Billings."

"Yes?" I turned back to him to see his eyes locked onto me. There was burning anger there that threw me back and put me in fear for my job.

"Since you seem to have a complete disregard for my rules, let me remind you. This is your job, not someplace to get your jollies on."

For a second, I thought he was talking about how I masturbated in the shower this morning. How the hell did he know I had done that? Did he have cameras or something in there? Out of all the outrageous things he could have done.

"Are you spying on me?" I snapped, horror filling my face. "How dare you? Just because I have to live here didn't mean you have the right to watch me in my private moments. Of all the fucking disturbing shi—"

"Enough." Antoine held a hand up. "I can assure you I have no idea what you are talking about. I couldn't care less about what you do in your private time. I'm talking about the rules you have been breaking."

My face burned for what felt like the hundredth time that day. He hadn't been spying on me while I rubbed one off to the thought of his brother. In fact, I had just told him I'd been doing just that thing. Then my embarrassment turned to anger when I understood what he was implying.

"Wait a second," I started again, realizing what he was talking about. "I'm not the one who's been trying to get their jollies on. I'm just doing my job."

"And breaking rules," Antoine shot back, "or did you not speak to me when you entered before I spoke to you?" He arched an elegant eyebrow, and I wanted to punch him in the face.

Crossing my arms over my chest, I frowned. "Well, excuse me if I find it common courtesy to let someone know what they are doing in their room. I'm only human."

Antoine's eyes scanned over my form, and he seemed to relax slightly. "Yes, so you are. However, in the future, I expect you to be seen and not heard. Preferably unseen as well. Then we won't have any of issues of boundaries being overstepped. Am I clear?"

My fingers curled into fists, and I pressed my lips together tight. Forcing back the rude remark that was dying to come out, I simply nodded.

"Good." Antoine turned his eyes back down to the papers in his hands before adding, "Good night, Miss Billings. Make sure you lock your door tonight."

As I left his room and headed back to my own, Antoine's words worried me. Were his brothers so hard up for female companionship that they would come into my room at night? Or was I being protected from something else? Either way, this job was getting weirder and weirder by the second. However, I was determined to be able to last until I could find another one.

If I could find another one.

CHAPTER 8

Drake

"YOU WANTED TO SEE me, brother?" I asked as I stepped into Antoine's office, having a feeling I knew what this meeting was about. Marcus was nothing more than Antoine's lapdog most days. Of course, he'd run to him the moment that delicious maid escaped my room.

Antoine sat behind his desk, his eyes down on the papers in front of him. He always had endless paperwork as the head of the house. I never knew what he actually had to do it all for. Antoine never offered up any information, so I never asked. Paperwork wasn't exactly my idea of a good time.

"Marcus has informed me of an incident with Miss Billings." The sharp tone to his voice told me it was a statement, not a question.

I dropped into the chair in front of his desk and threw my feet up on the edge of it. "I was just playing with her."

Antoine glanced up from the desk, his eyes going to my feet. Immediately, I dropped them to the floor with a thud.

"Regardless, didn't we make the agreement to leave this one alone? How is playing with her following that agreement?"

I scowled. "I didn't agree to anything. You told us to leave her alone. Besides, it's not like I used my powers on her or anything. I used my natural-born looks."

"Of that, I have no doubt." Antoine sat his pen down and steepled his fingers together. "I don't believe I made myself clear when I said no interference whatsoever. I meant to say that there will be no magical or physical shenanigans. We don't need another lovesick maid sneaking into the basement while looking for a bit of attention."

I grimaced. The last maid we had fell head over heels for Allister. She'd broken down the basement door and climbed into Allister's bed while we were sleeping. We didn't know she was there until dark had come.

My brother had a voice that could compel even the straightest man into dropping to his knees for him if Allister so much as whispered in his direction. Sometimes, I envy his abilities. They were much more effective than mine.

Vampires naturally had a charm to them, a compulsion if you will, that drew humans to us like moths to flames. My charm happened to be stronger than others, and I couldn't exactly turn it off. So, in close quarters like I'd been with Piper, it was easy to manipulate her into giving into me. However, since using our abilities on her was a big no-no, I'd had to rely on my other 'gifts.'

"Fine," I huffed. "I'll keep my gifts and every other extremity to myself."

"That's all I ask of you."

"Can I go now?" I stood even as I asked it.

Antoine waved me away, turning back to his papers. If there was a hell, then I knew I'd be filling out papers for eternity when my time came. Bless the poor bastard.

Before I made my escape, Antoine called out, "How did she take it?"

I hummed, turning back around. "Take what?"

"Your charm?"

I scrubbed a hand over my jaw and smirked. "Well, before your dog came barreling in, I almost had her."

Antoine quirked a brow. "And after?"

"She called me an asshole and stormed out." I chuckled and shook my head. That maid sure had a mouth on her. I didn't think much was going to spook her.

"Hmm."

"That's it?" I asked, my brow furrowed. "That's all you can say?"

Brushing his long braid over his shoulder, Antoine picked up his pen once more. "The donors will be here a bit later tonight than usual, so try not to make a spectacle of yourselves while waiting."

I puffed out a breath of air. "Fine, whatever."

Without permission, I threw open his office door and headed back to my room. Half way there, I detoured into my twin's room instead. I opened the door without knocking and found Allister reading a book. He was so engrossed by it, he hardly noticed me enter.

Coming up behind him, I snatched the book out of his hands and turned it over to read the cover. "The Art of Body Language? Really, Al?"

Scowling at me, Allister grabbed the book from my hand and scrambled for his page. "It's not easy seducing someone when your best feature is also the only way you know how to communicate."

I laughed and tossed myself onto his bed, lacing my hands behind my head. "You could pass notes? I'm sure she could decipher your chicken scratch if you were determined enough."

Allister snorted. "Easy for you to say, you don't have to speak to women to get them to fall for you." He nodded his head toward me.

"We're twins, dumbass. Any advantage I have in looks, you have as well." I leaned up on my elbows and stared at him. It was like looking at a mirror sometimes with our features were so exactly the same. However, years of comparing ourselves has made it easy to find our differences.

Where Allister had dimples in his cheeks, I had only the single one on the left side. My chin pointed a bit sharper compared to my brothers, and if I do say so myself, I had the bigger cock.

The subtle differences between us didn't stop there either. Even as children, before we became vampires, we had different tastes in everything from music to women. The fact that we both were interested in the maid was pure luck.

Or maybe it was our competitive nature? It was that competitive nature that had made us choose to be vampires in the first place. We were constantly trying to outdo the other. So, when we were busy showing off our strength and charm to the ladies of the seventeen-fifties, our sire found us.

He told us, "I am in need of a new companion, but I cannot bear to break up such a perfect set." And the rest was history. I doubted our parents ever expected us to live for as long as we did. They always thought we'd end up dying from some stupid dare or another.

"Do you ever think about our parents?" Allister asked out of the blue. It was freaky when he did that, like our minds were in tune with one another.

"I just was actually."

Allister clucked his tongue. "I wonder sometimes. If we hadn't been made into vampires, would we have lived much longer?"

I chortled. "I doubt it. You'd have dared me to jump of a bridge and—"

"Knowing you, you'd be stupid enough to do it." Allister smirked at me, then turned back to his book flipping through the pages.

Jumping off the bed, I smacked him on the back of the head. "Then you're even more of an idiot because you'd follow after me just to show you weren't a coward."

Laughing with me, Allister thunked his book down and collapsed back into his chair. "So, what did dear old Antoine want now? Did he give you a right talking to for playing with the maid?"

I leaned against his desk, not bothering to ask how he knew. "Pfft. Antoine has a stick so far up his ass, he'll need surgical assistance removing it."

"I think he just needs to get laid."

Pursing my lips, I thought about it. When was the last time I'd seen Antoine happy? It's been at least a decade or two. "He hasn't gotten any since that orgy in Prague."

Allister frowned. "It's been that long? No wonder he's wound so tight. Maybe Marcus should help him out a bit more than just being his lap dog."

Shaking my head, I shifted on the desk. "I don't think things have been that way between them for a while. Not since..." I trailed off, trying to think of when I'd last seen them touchy feely around each other.

"Dallas, I'm pretty sure," Allister answered for me.

"Really? That was fifty years ago. Surely they've bumped uglies between now and then?"

Allister shrugged. "I don't know. I make it a point to not be in either of their bedrooms. I prefer the company of women only."

"Thank fuck for that." Allister and I shared a laugh, before I paused with a thought. "Do you think this new maid would be against having brothers? Twins, specifically?"

Arching a brow, Allister asked, "Is this your way of saying you want to double team her?"

"Hey," I smirked, giving him a wink. "It can't hurt our odds."

CHAPTER 9

Piper

OF ALL THE DISGUSTING bullshit jobs I could land, I had to end up with this one. My nose wrinkled up as I scrubbed the inside of the toilet bowl of Wynn's bathroom. I'd already finished the others, this was my last room and to be honest, cleaning someone's toilet kind of took the edge off my attraction to him. Not all of it but a smidgen.

I blamed karma. I'd been too big of a bitch. Pissed off one too many people and now karma was back to bite me in the ass.

Sure, this job started out great. Big house, hot bosses, but then it progressively just got worse. I mean doing their laundry was one thing. At least none of them had skid marks in their underwear - not that I was checking mind you. And I had to say cleaning windows wasn't exactly a horrible job, I mean, it killed my back by the end of the day, but it wasn't as bad as having to clean the very thrones that these assholes sit on.

They weren't disgusting by any means but just the thought of cleaning them made me shudder. Now that I was in Wynn's bathroom, I wanted nothing more than to dig a hole and die.

Please don't suddenly need something from your room.

I'd been chanting the opposite of that thought over and over again as I picked up the gorgeous man's room but then the moment I had to get down on my hands and knees and put my hand in his toilet, I'd changed my tune.

Letting out a long drawn out sigh, I closed the lid of the toilet and tossed the cleaning brush into my bucket of supplies. "Fucking finished."

I used one hand to pull the rubber glove off the other and then grabbed the inside edge of the other to turn the gloves inside out. The last thing I needed was to spread germs all over the now clean bathroom. Plus, I had an issue with touching my face and I gagged at the thought of doing it with the gloves on.

Picking up my bucket, I started for the door. I didn't know why but for some reason I paused. I sat the bucket down and twisted on my heel, taking in Wynn's bedroom. I'd been in it several times but never had I snooped. Never had I had the urge to dig through his things and find out what made Wynn tick.

It would be wrong. An invasion of privacy.

Only if they catch you.

I let out a nervous giggle and spin around the room, trying to decide what to look at first. My eyes land on his dresser. Everyone knows the best place to hide things you didn't want anyone to find was in your dresser drawers. Especially the underwear drawer.

Practically skipping over to it, I pulled the top drawer open. Socks. Lots of socks. I dug a little deeper. I frowned. Well that sucked. There wasn't anything interesting in his sock drawer.

Shoving the top drawer closed I went to the next one. This one too held nothing of interest, just a bunch of t-shirts. The next few drawers lacked the same secrets and my excited quickly dwindled.

"Well, that sucks." I pursed my lips and tapped my finger against my chin, trying to think of where someone like Wynn might hide something valuable to him. My eyes land on his closet. "Ah, of course." I snapped my fingers and rushed over to the closet door.

Throwing it open, I took my time going through each and every item hanging up. After a moment or two, I found nothing. Nada. A bunch of expensive suits, ties, and belts. There wasn't even a balled up facial tissue in his pocket.

The only peculiar thing was a shirt that looked like it could be from the sixteen hundreds. Made out of white linen with a puffy collar and long sleeves, it would be perfect for a costume party or even one of those Renaissance fairs. The thought of Wynn going to one of those made me giggle. He'd have women throwing themselves over each other to give him their favors.

Not giving up hope of finding something embarrassing, I dropped to my knees and dug around the back of the closet. Even his shoes were nice and neat on a shoe rack, each of them made by some expensive company. There wasn't a tennis shoe among them though which was a bit odd but not exactly the kind of thing I was looking for.

"Maybe he doesn't have any skeletons in his closet." I muttered to myself, standing and closing the door. My eyes drift over to the bed and a small smile spread across my lips. "Maybe he hides them under the bed!"

Racing across the room, I didn't even pause to think about it before throwing myself onto his large four poster bed. Making a sort of snow angel movement, I rolled around on top of his comforter and pillows breathing in the scent of him. I could just imagine waking up in this bed with Wynn. Some mornings, I would wake before him and I'd roll over to kiss him awake.

Okay, if I was being honest with myself, I wouldn't stop at a kiss. In the movies someone always wakes up the other person with oral and I'd be lying if I didn't have a dark fantasy of doing that sometime and Wynn would be just the person that would enjoy that sort of thing.

None of my past boyfriends were very adventurous. Even in the bedroom. Sure, we might have tried out a few positions outside of the normal but it was always in the cover of darkness and under the blankets. I wondered for a second what that said about me and my taste in men. Did I always pick the ones that were safe? Predictable? And what did it say about me now that I was drooling all over a man's bed I just met - who for all intent and purposes was technically my boss?

"Great, Piper." I grumbled, sliding off the bed. "Way to be a creeper."

I went about fixing the comforter, remaking it so that it was smooth and untouched. Or at least looked it.

Then with little enthusiasm, I knelt on the ground and peeked beneath the bed skirt. Nothing but dust bunnies.

"If you're looking for my playboys, I don't keep them there."

With a startled sound, I jerked up. My gaze darted to the bedroom door where Wynn leaned against the frame a twinkle of amusement in his eyes. Clamoring to my feet, I dusted my jeans and t-shirt off. "I was just looking to see if I needed to clean under there."

"And do you?" Wynn asked, moving into the room. His long legs moved in a slow and lazy pace, his hands tucked into his pockets as if he had all the time in the world.

"Do I what?" I found myself gaping at him, my own feet slowing on the way to my discarded bucket.

Wynn chuckled, a sound that made my insides giddy. "Do you need to clean under my bed?"

I broke my eyes away from his and glanced back at the bed. My brow furrowed, I shook my head. "It's a bit dusty but I'll come back later and get under all of your beds. That way I can do it all at once."

When I turned my head back Wynn was right in front of me, barely a foot between us.

His eye lids drooped, and a small smile played at his lips. He reached out a hand toward me. I hated that I flinched. Even more so that he thought it was funny. Then he tucked a piece of my falling hair behind my ear. "I don't know if anyone has told you, but we really appreciate all the hard work you have done, Piper."

That single touch of his finger brushing my ear sent an electric current through my veins settling low between my thighs. I let out a gurgling sound, my knees threatening to give out on me. The second Wynn pulled his hand away the feeling was gone, and I could semi breathe again.

Embarrassed beyond relief, I swallowed hard and nodded stiffly. "Of course, it's my pleasure." I choked out the last word my face a flame at the wolfish grin on Wynn's lips as his hand touched my arm. Once more my knees seem to weaken, and an intense rush of desire raced through me. I almost orgasmed on the spot.

Shaking my head, I moved away from his touch and darted for the door. "I have to go clean something." It wasn't until I was half way down the stairs that I realized I'd forgotten my bucket of cleaning supplies.

CHAPTER 10

Wynn

A SMIRK ON MY lips, my eyes followed the sexy little maid as she practically ran out of my bedroom. Okay, so I might have cheated a bit but I barely even had to push my power into her and she almost fell apart on at the seams. I could only imagine how she'd react if I really gave it my all.

Chuckling to myself, I moved around my room looking for anything she might have found. I didn't make a habit of keeping my secrets in my bedroom. Not that I particularly had any outside of my powers and being a vampire. After several hundred years, one stopped being attached to materialistic things.

I opened my closet and took a deep breath. Piper was in here as well, her scent - a sweet mixture of lilacs and honey - covered the clothing inside. One item in particularly had her scent all over it.

Frowning, I pulled out the shirt I'd kept all these years. When our sire found me, I'd been a playboy in Vienna. Spending my father's money and hiding beneath women's skirts. It didn't matter to me if they were attached or otherwise. I wanted nothing more than to get drunk and get my cock wet. Unfortunately, my father had other plans for me.

He'd wanted me to grow up and take over the family business. However, I'd never been one for politics. Or being serious for that matter. All that ass kissing and playing by the rules were never my style. Which was why I didn't care that I'd already cheated Antoine's ban on using my powers.

Besides, who was she going to tell? For all Piper knew, she was just extremely attracted to me. I bet if I chased after her, I'd find her hiding away somewhere with her fingers down her panties. The thought of it made me hard.

Jesus fuck.

The way her full luscious lips had parted as my powers raced over her, I'd almost said fuck it and thrown her on my bed and showed her how exactly we appreciated her hard work. She was so responsive. So innocent. The little human maid might have been with men before but not the way I wanted her. No, if I had the chance, I'd show her the finer points of pleasure. How sometimes being teased just to the edge was just as good as the real thing.

I groaned and adjusted myself in my pants, my hard on getting worse.

Moving away from the closet, I followed the trail of her scent to the immaculate bathroom. She really was a great maid. I'd give her that. Even if I'd rather she her on her knees before me than cleaning a toilet.

From the bathroom, I walked over to my bed. What she had thought she'd find underneath it was beyond me. Who kept things under there? It would be the first place anyone would look. All of my private things were locked away in a safety deposit box or were down in the basement by my day time resting place. Some place I should be right now with the rest of my brothers, but I couldn't stop hearing her moving around up here. I had to see what Piper was up to.

Stopping by my bed, I frowned. My eyes narrowed on the covers which looked undisturbed, but my nose said otherwise. Placing a knee up on the bed, I climbed onto it. My nostrils flared as I picked up her heady scent. She'd laid on my bed. More than that, she'd practically rubbed herself all over it like some kind of cat in heat. Laying down in the spot she had laid on, I trailed a hand over my stomach.

Just the thought of the blonde maid on my bed made me want to rush out of the room and bring her back. It was quite obvious that even without my powers, she wanted me and who was I to tell a beautiful woman no? I'd never done it before, why start now?

Because Antoine would punish you.

Oh, but it would be worth it.

The last time I remembered having a woman this intriguing near me was right before my sire found me. I'd been with the Count of Mansfeld's wife. I let out a laugh. That day had been more entertaining than any of my days in my undead life. The countess and I had been mid-coitus when her husband showed up. I'd climbed out of the bedroom window in the middle of the day and had to out run a pack of dogs the count had sic'd on me.

What a night. There hadn't been a woman that much of a challenge since then. They all fell head over heels in love with me the moment they met me. The few times they hadn't, all I needed to do was push a bit of my power into them and they were putty in my hands.

Piper wanted me though. I could tell. However, she hadn't tried to climb into bed with me or even kiss me. Perhaps, she had more self-restraint than the others?

Pfft. I shook my head and sat up. She'd fall just like everyone else. No one was that interesting anymore.

Walking across the room, I headed for the door. I'd been up far too long as it was, the day time wasn't a pleasant time for those of my kind. It wasn't that we couldn't be awake, but we were nocturnal creatures. Everything in our bodies screamed at us to hide and sleep in the dark. The sun was the enemy. The cruelest and least merciful of any enemy we'd ever had.

Even the vampire hunters could be persuaded to leave us be after a bit, but the sun would never hear our words. Or if it did, how could one stop being what it was for the sake of others?

A philosophical thought for another day.

Passing by the bucket Piper had left, I almost grabbed it. Then with a sly grin sat it back down. Let her gather the courage to come back to my room. If I was lucky, I'd be there to catch her again. This time though, I wasn't sure I'd be able to play by the rules.

CHAPTER 11

Piper

THE NEXT FEW DAYS were pretty much all the same. I got up, found the note shoved under my door, and started the day. Some days, Gretchen would serve me breakfast, other days, I'd make my own. Darren rarely sat with me at meals, and when he did, he didn't talk to me much, no matter how much I tried.

"Why, you look absolutely thrilled to be here," Rayne said as he plopped down on the stairs next to where I was scrubbing a stain from the floor.

I had finished all my chores early and had been looking forward to a nice relaxing evening instead of collapsing in my bed. However, God hated me.

Darren had stopped me in the kitchen and told me of a mysterious red stain that had suddenly appeared. As the maid, of course, it was my job to get rid of it. Since I wasn't exactly an expert in tile cleaning, I had been scrubbing at the same spot for over an hour, and still, the ugly red spot had hardly budged.

"Can I help you?" I sighed and tossed my scrubbing brush back into my bucket of water.

Rayne smirked down at me, his hands laced in front of him as he leaned on his knees. "No, just enjoying your pitiful existence."

Rolling my eyes, I turned back to my bucket and grimaced at the reddish colored water. I'd gotten this much stuff out of the tile, but still, it glared at me like a neon light. Suddenly, a thought came to mind. I glanced at Rayne's overly smug face and then back to the stain.

"You did this, didn't you?" I arched a brow at him, ready for a reason to smack him upside the head like he deserved.

Annoying punk.

Leaning back on the stairs, Rayne sniggered. "Now, why would I do that? I have so many other more important things to do than to make more work for you."

I snorted. "Yeah, like I believe that."

Standing up, Rayne stomped over to where I knelt and crouched down beside me. "You should watch your tongue unless you want to be out of a job and back to living in your car."

I gaped at him. "How did you know that?"

"I have my ways." When I only stared at him, he sighed. "It's called the Internet. I did a background check on you. You've been job hopping for the last few months after you got laid off." His nose scrunched up in disgust. "Also, your car is a mess. You should take more pride in your things."

Why, that snot-nosed little brat. Who did he think he was?

Irritation filled me, and I jumped to my feet. "And you should mind your own business. What I do or don't do with my own stuff is my business, not yours." I huffed and picked up my bucket of water, glaring down at him. "If you ever do something like this again, I will make sure all your clothes are dyed pink in the next wash."

I whipped back around, making sure the water in the bucket sloshed over the side and splashed Rayne's feet.

"Hey!" Rayne jumped back and snarled. "Watch it. You better come back here and apologize. You're nothing but a maid."

"And you're nothing but a spoiled brat," I snapped back at him, flipping him off. I marched back toward the kitchen, muttering to myself the entire way.

I might be a maid, but that didn't give him the right to treat me like shit. I worked hard to clean their clothes and keep their ridiculously large house clean. Really, who needed this many rooms? There were only six of them and way too much unused square footage to need this big of a house.

I slammed my bucket down on the counter a bit more forcefully than needed.

Darren stood at the stove, his back to me as he stirred a pot on the burner. He glanced away from the pot for a moment to arch a brow. "Bad day?"

I grunted and went to the sink. Dumping the water into the sink, I twisted toward Darren, one hip leaned against the counter. "Tell me, did all these guys personally shove sticks up their asses or were they born that way?"

"I wouldn't speak so freely of the masters," Darren warned though I caught a hint of a smile on his lips. "They have excellent hearing."

I sniffed, not at all worried. "Then hear this, bite me!"

Darren chuckled, his shoulders shaking with the effort. He went back to stirring the delicious smelling pot. Remarkably, not even the prospect of food made up for my day.

"What, you think that's funny?" I spat, staring at him like he had lost his mind.

"Just your wording. The irony." Darren shook his head and then started to plate the food. He gestured to the bar for me to sit.

I flopped into my seat and forked up the pasta creation in front of me, but I was so mad that I couldn't even get any into my mouth. I threw my fork back down and growled. "These guys are the worst pains in the asses I've ever come across. If they aren't trying to embarrass me, they're trying to break my back with the amount of work they give me."

"So, quit if you hate it so much," Darren answered. Besides, I'm the one who writes your list of chores. Maybe it should be me you hate."

He had a point. However, writing a list didn't make him an asshole, not like that little, redheaded jerk face.

"I can't hate you. You're just doing what you're told. Just like me."

Darren made a huff of confirmation.

"As far as quitting," I glared down at my plate, and my lower lip poked out on its own accord, "I would if I could. However, jobs aren't that easy to come by with my track record."

I wish Rayne had been lying, but he hadn't. I'd like to say that it was the jobs. Each job I had gotten from the temp agency had been one piece of shit assignment after the other. But to be honest, it was me. When I first lost my cushy job and started at the agency, I'd been picky. Too picky. I turned down too many good jobs because I thought I was better than that.

I'd been wrong.

Now, I counted my blessings for this job. The pay was reasonable even if it didn't come with health care or dental. However, I could afford to save for any mishaps with what I saved from living at the job. It sure beat the hell out of living in my car. More comfortable too.

I turned my attention back to Darren. The company wasn't half bad either, the couple of jerk face masters aside.

"So, I heard." Darren inclined his head. "Living in your car, huh?" He raised his brows at me, pity in his eyes. "It takes quite a bit to drive someone to those lengths."

I shrugged, stabbing at my noodles but not really trying to eat them. "Not really. It made sense with the lack of funds to pay for an apartment."

"What about your parents?" Darren asked, surprising me. This was the longest conversation I'd ever had with Darren. The fact that he was even asking me about myself was a miracle. Usually, he was trying his best to get me out the door or back to work.

"They're not here, and even if they were, I wouldn't go back to them." I left it at that, not wanting to go into my family history.

"So, you're here on your own with no family to look for you?" Darren asked a bit strangely. "That's not a safe place to be for a young woman."

I shifted in my seat uncomfortably. "I can take care of myself."

Darren snorted. "That I can't believe."

We continued to eat in silence after Darren's condescending remark. I wanted to argue that I was perfectly capable of taking care of myself, but the memory of how easily Drake had overtaken me. How close I'd been to letting him take me up against his bedroom door.

I wasn't a large woman. I wasn't petite either. If it came down to brute strength, I couldn't hold my own against even Rayne, the smallest of them. Though the thought of Wynn overcoming me wasn't an unpleasant thought, I wouldn't want to be at the mercy of that brat.

Darren took both of our plates before I could offer to clean them and then disappeared into the dining room. A few low voices came from there, and I was half tempted to see if my employers were there. What did they eat? So, far I hadn't seen them get anything remotely close to food besides Rayne's bottle of red crap.

Suddenly, Darren showed back up in the kitchen. His eyes landed on me, and he stiffened. "You should go to bed. The masters have some visitors tonight, and they don't want to be disturbed."

The tone of his voice told me there was no room for argument. The voices in the dining room got louder, and there were laughter and some moaning noises. Suddenly, I wanted to be back in my room.

As I scrambled up the back stairs, my face heated. What kind of people was I working for? Nymphomaniacs? Maybe one of those BDSM kind of groups?

They did want to be called Master.

Whips and chains came to mind as well as the image of Antoine in some assless leather pants. My body shivered deliciously at the thought. I could totally see any of them being into that kind of stuff.

I paused at my bedroom door and was half tempted to head back down, but Darren's warning look before had taken all my courage. Turning the knob, I ducked inside just as a loud cry of ecstasy filled the house.

Yeah, I was going with sex-addicts.

Laying in my bed that night, I had a hard time sleeping. All I could think about was what was going on downstairs. Eventually, after several hours of tossing and turning in my lovely sheets, I climbed out of bed and inched toward my door. I pressed my ear to the wood of the door and listened.

Nothing.

Opening the door, I poked my head out into the hallway. When I didn't hear anything, I stepped out of my room. I stood there for longer than I should have, waiting for something or someone to attack me or whatever it was that Darren and the rest had warned me against.

I laughed a bit at my silliness, shaking my head.

Heading down the stairs to the kitchen, I thought of the batch of cookies I'd seen Gretchen hide up in the cabinet early today. That's what I needed after a shit day, a glass of milk and a big fat cookie. Sounded like a nice treat to me.

With a little shimmy in my step, I made my way around the island and over to the cabinet. I reached up and tried to reach behind the box of macaroni, searching for those cookies. My fingers just about got them when a low moan drifted into the kitchen, freezing me in place.

I dropped back onto my heels and spun around, my eyes darting toward the entrance of the dining room. Were they really still at it? I waited, my ears peeled for another sound, but nothing came. Must have been my imagination.

Still, I didn't waste any more time. I climbed up onto the counter and grabbed the container of cookies. With a happy grin on my face, I began to turn around.

"You know, it's dangerous to be climbing on counters like that."

My socked foot slipped on the marble countertop as my eyes shot up to see, Rayne leaning against the door to the dining room. I let out a startled shout and threw my hands up to catch myself. The cookies flew from my hand and spun through the air as my eyes squeezed shut.

Instead of crashing onto the marble, my body slammed into a pair of strong arms.

Gasping, my eyes flew open. Light brown met amber. My heart threatened to jump out of my chest, and the sniggering grin on Rayne's lips made me scowl. Shoving at his arms, I dropped my feet to the ground.

"Don't do that," I snapped, smacking him on the arm.

Rayne only grinned in amusement at my violence. "I told you it was dangerous."

"Yes, but whose fault is that?" I bent down and searched for the cookie container. Finally finding it, I climbed back to my feet with a happy squeal.

"All that for a couple of cookies?"

My exasperated eyes slid in his direction. "You obviously haven't had Gretchen's cookies."

Rayne's lips tipped down. "Of course, I have. They're not worth breaking your neck."

I lifted a shoulder and dropped it, popping the lid off to snag one of those cookies. Taking a large bite of it, I closed my eyes briefly. "Hmmm. Yep. Worth it." I gave him a sly grin which he returned with a curious stare. I started for the stairs and then paused, my socked foot sliding on the floor as I turned back around. "Why did you save me? I thought you couldn't wait to get rid of me. If I had broken my neck, you'd have had your wish."

Shifting from one foot to the other, Rayne moved over to the island and leaned on the top of the counter. He gestured a hand toward the container. I hesitated but then figured they were technically his by right. Moving over to the island, I slid the container across the table, leaning on my own side so that we were across from each other. I watched him with wary eyes, taking another bite of my cookie.

Snagging a cookie for himself, Rayne bit into it. Unlike me, he didn't coo and moan at the taste, he actually didn't seem to care for it at all. Weird.

Licking his lips, Rayne met my gaze. "If you die, we'd get another maid, one who might be even more pathetic than you. At least, you aren't falling all over yourself trying to get into my brothers' beds."

I forced myself not to react. I'd only really thought about getting into one of the brothers' beds, Wynn, and that was only in my mind. I'd never try and sneak into his bed.

Shaking my head, I grabbed the cookie container back from his ungrateful clutches. "I need this job, as you know." I sneered at him before spinning away.

Halfway up the stairs, he called out to me. "Remember that when you have your fingers deep inside of your pussy tonight."

I chunked a cookie at his head and didn't wait for his laughter to follow me up the stairs on the way back to my room. Stupid ass hat.

CHAPTER 12

Rayne

MY FANGS PIERCED THE skin of the blonde woman in my lap. She wiggled but didn't complain. My cock stiffened at the friction.

I didn't usually go for blondes. They were too frivolous and chipper. Give me a good brunette with wit and a smart mouth. However, a certain blonde creature had taken up residence in my head and I couldn't shake her.

Piper Billings wasn't like the others. She didn't giggle or bat her eyes at me or my brothers. All the maids had fallen all over themselves to get close to us.

Especially Wynn. They just couldn't help themselves. It wasn't his fault really. Okay, fuck that it was completely his fault. He didn't know how to keep his eyes and mouth to himself. Then there was that damn power in his touch.

I'd give up being able to hear others' thoughts for being able to make someone orgasm with just a touch. Then again, he had more control than I did over his ability. I couldn't stop hearing that little blonde-haired maid's thoughts. Not only did she talk to herself way too much, but she was giving me the worst case of blue balls I'd ever had, and I was thirty years undead!

Sadly, it wasn't surprising that out of the six of us, he was the one on her mind the most. I tried not to peek into too many of the help's heads, some things were best kept in the dark, but Piper was... peculiar. She wanted us, that much I knew. She even found me attractive despite how much she bitched at me.

However...

She never acted on it, at least not outside of her room in the cover of night. Unfortunately for her, that was the time we were awake the most.

God. The way she moaned. The images in her head. It had each of us staring holes in the ceiling of the basement.

"Is something wrong?" *He's cute, bite's a bit lazy though. Give me a good hard bite any day.*

I forced myself not to grimace at her thoughts though she had a point. I hadn't even noticed I'd stopped biting her until my donor said something. Fuck. What was Piper doing to me?

I glanced up at the woman with the pretty blue eyes. The wrong color. They should be brown, a light chestnut color with a fire burning beneath the iris.

Wiping a hand across my mouth, I shook my head. "Sorry, babe. I must not be hungry."

The woman pouted, her thin lips not the ones I wanted to look at. I trailed a hand down her back, and then gave her a nudge. "Go on. I'm sure someone else would be happy to have you."

She slid off my lap and sauntered across the room. Allister crooked his finger at her, having already taken his share from his donor. The greedy bastard. The blonde didn't seem to mind, she licked her lips and gave him a flirty smile before climbing into her lap.

I wanted the big one anyway.

Fucking slut.

Sighing, I stood from my chair. I dragged a hand through my shaggy hair. Maybe I'll go out. Take a walk. Maybe hunt someone down for a change. Having a service bring our donors was easier, more discreet, but it took away the best part about being a vampire. The danger. The excitement.

Neutered. That's what we were.

"What bug crawled up your ass?" Drake glanced up from his donor, a gorgeous red head with large breasts, blood dripping down his lips. Her dress barely covered them, and Drake had taken advantage of all the bare skin, littering her chest with bites. They'd heal by morning if he did his job right.

"Just not hungry," I grumbled, not looking to deal with the thoughts inside my head as well as his.

Don't stay out too late.

I flipped him the bird on my way out of the dining room. I glanced at the front door tempted to go out, but something called me up the stairs. I knew where I was headed and yet I couldn't stop myself from going.

At the top of the stairs, Antoine's voice stopped me instead. "You should leave her alone."

Not turning to face him, I stared down the dark hallway. "She thinks more than any maid we've ever had. Should have gotten another dumb one. She's not likely to stay in the dark for long."

Antoine scoffed. "You wouldn't say that had you not woken up with one of those bumbling idiots in your day time bed." He paused for a moment, his mind recapturing the time he talked about. That maid had been lucky he hadn't killed her on the spot. She had been sent packing right then and there.

That had been our last maid. Now, Piper.

I wasn't unaware enough not to realize I wanted her, nor did I deny it. However, I didn't know how to get her to like me like the other maids did. She wasn't easy. I should be happy for a challenge after all my years, but all I could think about was how frustrating all of it was. How frustrating she was.

"Make sure you don't let anyone see you tonight."

"Huh?" I glanced back at Antoine, forgetting he was even there.

"You are going out tonight, yes?" Antoine tossed his white hair over his shoulder, his pale eyes sharp and all seeing in the dark. Not much got by Antoine. Probably why he was the head of the house. He could have it. Too much drama and political bullshit came with that job.

"Uh, yeah. In a bit. Gotta get something out of my room."

Antoine nodded and walked back into the dining room.

Without an audience, I stepped onto the landing of the second floor. I shifted toward my room, I should go. Antoine was usually right. Fucking asshole. I was the telepath, I should be right at least ninety percent of the time. At least, I should be right more than him.

Screw it.

He wasn't the boss of me. If I wanted to fuck with the maid, I would. Not like she even had any interest in me anyway. Her mind was full of Wynn.

Stomping across the landing to the servants' wing, I bypassed Darren's room. The serious butler wasn't in his room anyway. He would still be down stairs, waiting to see if we needed anything. He didn't sleep much from what I could tell. Strange for a human though, with his blood bond to us, he was hardly human anymore.

Not like Piper.

Stopping in front of her door, I reached for the door handle. I twisted it. Locked. Raising my hand to knock on the door, I paused at a sound. A low breathy moan creeped through the door. Shifting closer to the wood, I pressed my ear to the surface.

There it was again. Definitely a moan. Was she touching herself again?

I must be a glutton for punishment because I reached out for her thoughts without hesitation. Her mind was fuzzy, telling me that she was dreaming. However, the maid might as well be flicking her bean for the images inside her head.

Piper sat on the island in the kitchen, her body bare and her legs spread wide as Wynn slammed into her pussy. She had her head thrown back as she cried out in pleasure. In her mind's eye, I could see her breasts in perfect clarity. The rosy tips of her nipples made my mouth water and my fangs ache. I wanted to see more, but even I felt like a pervert, standing here peeping on her mind.

I grunted, reaching down to adjust myself. Even with Wynn as the main attraction, the sight of her body and sound of her moans were almost too much for me. I started to pull away from her thoughts, dead set on finding a willing woman outside of the house for the night when her dream changed.

While Wynn had her front half, another set of hands slid over her shoulders. A familiar head of hair bent over her neck, placing open-mouthed kisses along her throat. I gaped. Piper actually dreamed of me?

"Anything good?"

I jerked away from the door to see a smirking Wynn standing a few feet away. Turning my eyes from his, I cleared my throat. "Not a thing."

"Sure, didn't look like it. You're about to bust your load right outside of our sweet maid's door." Wynn pointed his finger at my hard on.

"Fuck you," I snapped, glaring at him. Hands curled into fists, I stomped away from the room, shoving my shoulder against Wynn's.

Big mistake.

A shock of pleasure ran through me. Groaning, I doubled over, and my hand shot out to grab the nearest thing which happened to be Wynn himself. I swallowed and gasped, trying to catch my breath as my orgasm shook through my body.

"What the fuck?" I gasped, ripping my hand away from the smirking bastard.

Wynn brushed his hand across his shoulder with a knowing grin. "You should mind your manners. Next time, I'll make sure she's here to watch."

CHAPTER 13

Piper

I SPENT THE REST of the night imagining what was going on down there. I'd never imagined any of them would be into that kind of stuff. Okay, that was a lie. I totally could see some BDSM action coming from a few of them.

But Rayne? He was a punk that seemed more like a bottom than a top. Wynn, oh, Wynn, I would let him tie me up any day. The thought of a twin sandwich also didn't strike me as something I would hate.

I was having a delicious dream of just those things when a pounding sounded on my door. Groaning, I glanced over at my clock. It was barely after seven. I was usually up by now, but apparently, I needed the sleep. Something I wished the person at my door would respect.

"Piper, get up," Darren's voice called out, making me groan again. Of course, it would be him, the freaking slave driver.

"I'm coming! Hold on a second." I crawled out of bed and pulled a pair of sweatpants on, not bothering to put a bra on under my big t-shirt. I pulled open the door to find an annoyed Darren waiting on the other side. "Yes?"

Darren's eyes dipped down slightly to my attire, and I could tell he didn't approve. Not voicing his opinion, he glanced to his wrist and his watch. "No list today. The masters are throwing a party. We need to get the house ready for visitors."

I frowned, my brow furrowing. "But they had visitors last night, and we didn't have to prepare anything."

Tapping his foot, Darren let out an exasperated sigh. "That was different. Today, we prepare the house, and tonight, you will stay in your room or, better yet, go visit a friend. You don't want to be caught up in their shenanigans. Now, get dressed and meet me in the kitchen. We have a lot of work to do."

Closing the door, I proceeded to do as he asked.

What kind of people have two parties in one week? The rich kind, obviously. Except it seemed like this time, it would be a bigger affair. What about Darren's comment? I understood the whole stay in my room bit. I was the help, no one wanted to see the help hanging around while they were trying to get their freak on.

However, asking me to leave the house altogether? That was a bit strange.

Trying not to think about it too much, I brushed my teeth and cleaned my face before heading downstairs. Gretchen was in the kitchen, cooking something that was not breakfast for me. On the table was a box of donuts with my name on it. Not literally but I could hear it singing out to me.

Eat me, Piper. You know you want to. We taste so good.

Sighing as I took a seat, I bit into the pastry. I really needed to get a life, one outside of work.

"Make sure you eat plenty this morning." Gretchen raised a brow at me. "If you think they have been working you hard now, you haven't seen their parties."

I slid my gaze over to Darren. The bastard ratted me out. Was nothing sacred in this house? Apparently not. I was on my own after all.

After I finished eating and drinking a whole pot of coffee, I turned to Darren. "So, boss, what's on the agenda for today? Maybe painting the whole mansion? Or cooking dinner for one hundred in one day?"

Gretchen snorted. "You leave the cooking to me, and if they ever gave me that short of notice for a hundred people, I would quit on the spot."

"Oh, no, you wouldn't," Darren shot back with a pointed look.

Gretchen sighed. "You're right, I wouldn't, but I would spank some butts!" She and Darren laughed heartily. I could tell they had been together a long time. They even had their own private jokes. I half wanted to be in on those jokes, but I also didn't want to be a maid for the rest of my life.

Their laughter cut off when Antoine showed up in the doorway of the kitchen. He nodded at Darren and then smiled at Gretchen. "Good morning, Miss Gretchen. Could you please add two more people to the place settings for this evening? The two we thought weren't coming have changed their minds."

"Of course, Master Durand." Gretchen smiled back at him like a grandmother would her grandson. It was a bit endearing had I not thought Antoine was a bit of an ass. A hot one, sure, but an ass none the less.

"Miss Billings." The tone of his voice changed from courteous to stern. "I expect Darren has told you about tonight's event. Everything must be perfect, so try not to break anything or antagonize any of my brothers today." I flushed as I realized he was talking about my encounter with Rayne yesterday. "We're all a bit on edge, and I can't be held responsible if something should happen to you."

I couldn't tell if Antoine was worried for me or just didn't want to be bothered by an incident. Either way, I got the message. Keep my head down, do my job, and stay out of the way.

"Understood, Master Durand." I nodded and then waited for Antoine to leave so I could finish eating the one good thing that had happened to me this week.

Antoine, however, didn't leave. He put his hands behind his back and strolled toward me. Gretchen and Darren seemed to hold their breath as Antoine moved into my personal space. He stopped at the island and leaned onto the counter next to me just inches from where I sat.

"I also wanted to be sure we have an understanding of a different matter." His face was so close to mine, it was strange and exciting. It made special tingles go through my body, and I had the sudden urge to lean toward him and bask in his scent. "Please refrain from speaking ill of my brothers and me in such a public setting. If you have any complaints, I expect you to handle them professionally and not scream them at the top of your lungs."

When I realized last night's 'Bite me!' was what he had been talking about, my face burned with embarrassment. Darren had been right about their hearing all right. I should have been more careful.

"I'm sorry. I didn't mean anything by it—"

Antoine's fingers covered my lips startling me. "Enough. I simply wish to remind you to think before you speak, because the next time you tell someone to bite you..." He leaned forward until I could feel his breath on my face. "... someone just might."

With that, Antoine was gone, and I was trying to relearn how to breathe. Glancing between Gretchen and Darren, who looked amused by the whole situation, I cried out. "What the fuck was that?"

Darren and Gretchen breathed out, visibly relaxing after Antoine left. Taking in a deep breath, Darren shook his head. "I hate to say I told you so but..."

Gretchen barked a laugh. "You big fibber, you love to say I told you so. Especially to anyone who isn't you." She waved her spatula in his direction with a roll of her eyes.

Straightening out, Darren tugged on the cuffs of his gloves. If it were possible his nose was stuck even further up in the air than ever before. "Regardless. I expect Piper to be more aware of her surroundings and save her outbursts for her days off," he locked those stern brown eyes with mine, his brows furrowing, "when you are out of the house."

I jerked my head up and down twice before shoving my donut into my mouth. With a little moan of relief, I sagged in my chair.

Darren watched me with a mixture of disgust and amusement before asking, "Are you finished? We have several items on today's agenda, and I would like to have them finished before the first guests arrive."

Slugging back what was left of my coffee mug, I gave him a thumbs up. "Let's go, boss."

Snorting, Darren adjusted his suit jacket. "Hardly." He left the kitchen through the dining room, not waiting for me to follow him.

Gretchen and I exchanged a knowing smile before I handed her my coffee mug and went after our stuck-up butler. I followed him into the dining room. The long dining table had been scrubbed clean recently, and the cleaning fluid stung my nose and made me sneeze.

They must have really made a mess last night.

"Come now, don't dally." Darren poked his head back into the dining room from the foyer. "We have plenty to do and not near enough time to do it."

Hurrying after him, I laced my finger behind my back. "So, how many people do you think will be coming? Is there a theme for this party?"

"Yes." Darren stopped before the hallway closet where he pulled out a long hook. Apprehension filled me as he came toward me with the hook. However, he stepped around me and hooked it into the rings of the heavy curtains over the windows. Light flooded into the room, and I held my hand up to block my eyes.

Blinking rapidly to get the spots out of my eyes, I searched for Darren's form. "Am I allowed to know the theme?" I huffed, my hands on my hips as I tapped my foot. "How can I help if I don't know what I'm doing?"

Darren finished pulling back all the drapes and clacked the end of the hook's pole on the ground. "You are not going to help with anything. We don't need to lose any more of our precious antiques to your clumsiness. The masters have hired decorators, and they will take care of everything."

"Then what am I supposed to do?" I crossed my arms over my chest, annoyance pinching my face.

Darren walked calmly to my side, the large hook looking over us. "You will stay out of sight. Take an early day off. Go get a manicure. Whatever it is you do with your free time, but don't come back until just before sunset." He started to walk away but then stopped. "Actually, if you could stay the night somewhere, maybe with a friend or a lover? That would be best for everyone."

"Then why did you even wake me up?" I snapped, marching after him before he could leave me behind. I followed him into the back of the house where a large library sat. I hadn't had a chance to go in there yet. None of my chores had asked me to, and there was never any time to explore.

Large shelves covered every wall of the library with a balcony wrapping around the second story. A rolling ladder was attached to a metal bar which moved all around the room. Desks and couches littered the room, but unlike most libraries, I'd seen no book was out of place. They were all neatly stacked on the shelves. No messy readers in this house.

Darren threw open the doors and began to pull the curtains back in there as well. "I have too much to do to wait for you to roll out of bed. Better to send you on your way now, so you are out of our hair."

A low growl erupted from my throat. "What's the point of being the maid if I can't do my job? You won't tell me anything. I'm already under contract to keep my mouth shut, but I can't keep quiet if I don't know what I'm being quiet about."

Throwing an irritated scowl over his shoulder, Darren finished the drapes and then strolled toward me. I thought he might ignore me once more, but instead, he stopped before me.

"You may think your role here is important, but you aren't. I cannot tell you anything until the masters deem you trustworthy enough to know. As for your job, you will be given more responsibility—"

"When I'm trusted enough to handle it," I filled in for him. "Yeah, yeah. Whatever." I waved him off and sighed. "Fine but I don't have anyone to stay with, so I'll just call it a night early. Will that be satisfactory?" I gave him a beaming 'fuck you' smile.

Darren sniffed. "If you must, but it is imperative your door be locked tonight. No late night snacks. No sneaking out to spy on the party. This is a very important night for Master Wynn, and we can't have you ruining it with your clumsy ways."

Master Wynn? If Darren had been trying to detract me from wanting to check out the party, he shouldn't have mentioned Wynn. Now I wanted to know what was going on even more than before.

Holding one hand up in front of me, I smiled innocently. "Promise. I'll be out until sunset."

"And?"

Putting my other hand behind my back, I crossed my fingers. "And I'll go straight to my room and stay there until sun up."

"Good. Now, get out of here." He brushed past me and then paused at the library door. "Clean your car, Lord knows it needs to be sanitized."

I glared at his retreating figure. Clean my car, my ass. My car was fine. Sure, it had been a pit for my many fast food wrappers, but that had changed. I now had a home to litter with those.

When I made my way out of the house and into my car, my nose wrinkled at the sour smell. Okay, so a car wash wouldn't be so bad after all.

CHAPTER 14

Antoine

DARREN STOOD IN THE doorway of my office. Annoyance covered his face. Not that it was much different than his usual look. The human servant's face always was sort of pinched, like it would kill him to be happy.

"What is it?" I tried not to snap at him but really the more time I spent being bothered the longer it would take to finish my work.

You'd think being undead would mean my life was full of blood and lounging about, but life still went on and the world was constantly changing. However, one thing never changed.

Paperwork.

It was unending it seemed. Like my life. I swore if a stake didn't kill me first, the paperwork would. It wasn't as bad as it used to be. The work took twice as long before computers and pens, back when everything had to be written by hand and the ink got everywhere. I'd ruined many a shirt because of ink spills.

I missed the good old days when one could make agreements and buy property by word of mouth and money. Nowadays, you needed lawyers and contracts. Too many people had no honor and would fuck you in the ass if you let them. I tried to be the fucker over the fuckee.

"I sent Miss Billings on a shopping trip as requested." Darren half bowed to me, his words pulling me from my thoughts.

"Good," I commented, tapping my pen on the top of my desk. "She needs to spend more time out of this house."

Darren's face pinched even more. It was going to implode if he didn't stop worrying so much. "But Master Durand, wouldn't it be wiser to keep her isolated? She would be less likely to tell secrets of the household if we keep her here."

I sighed and leaned back in my chair. "Normally, yes. However, this one has too many of my brothers intrigued."

"Probably because she hasn't tried to jump any of them in the hallways." Darren almost smiled, his lips tugging up at the sides.

"Yes, that might be it exactly. I thought having a maid who wasn't interested in us and desperately needed the job would make our lives easier but unfortunately..." I groaned and threw down my pen.

Darren moved across the room on his own, stopping beside my desk. I pushed my chair back slightly and gestured for him to come around.

Darren was blood bonded to me and, with that, came a certain attraction. Neither one of us particularly cared for men, but nonetheless, we wanted to touch each other, to make the other person feel better, in any way that was needed. Kneeling before me, Darren reached for the buttons of my pants.

"If she finds a social life outside of the house, then we are less likely to have to hire a new one any time soon," I explained. Thinking of the maid and her mouthy tendencies had me hardening beneath Darren's hands.

"She is a pretty thing," Darren commented, releasing me from my pants.

His hand wrapped around me, tugging on my length until I was thick and firm. Swirling his thumb over the head of my cock, Darren shifted closer to me. I parted my thighs allowing him room to fit between them, my anticipation building.

"Yes, she is," I hummed and then let out a sharp breath.

Darren pulled me into his mouth, the hot cavern making me grunt. One hand dipped into my pants, cupping me from beneath as his mouth worked me. I closed my eyes briefly and enjoyed the feel of his tongue curling around me, sliding up and down the sensitive flesh. Blonde hair and a pouty mouth came to my mind, and I could feel the edge coming closer than normal. I laid my hand on his head, moving him how I liked it. After all these years, Darren didn't need much instruction, and before long, I was coming.

Moving away, Darren wiped his mouth and buttoned my pants back up. "The preparations are almost complete. Would you like me to let you know when the guests arrive?"

I placed a hand against the side of his face. Stroking my fingers along the smooth skin of his cheek, I asked a question rather than answering his. "Do you enjoy your life here with us?"

Black brows shot to his hairline as Darren's eyes widened. "Of course, I do. You saved me. I am nothing but grateful to you. To all of you." He paused for a moment and then stood, adjusting his suit jacket. "Why do you ask?"

Twisting my chair back to my desk, I picked my pen back up. "No reason. Simply making sure your quality of life is still up to your standards. I would hate to have my best worker leave me all of a sudden." My lips curled up in a salacious grin. "After all, good help is so hard to find these days."

CHAPTER 15

Piper

I COULD HEAR THE party downstairs from my bedroom. The music beat through the floorboards, making it impossible to ignore it. Obviously, since I was the help, I wasn't invited. However, that didn't stop me from wanting to sneak a peek.

Flipping the page of my book, I forced myself to stare at the pages even though I wasn't really getting any of the story in. The book was some paranormal romance about vampires and werewolves, something that wouldn't happen in the real world, and I couldn't get into it, not when I had my very own set of panty-dropping men to daydream over.

Giving up, I threw the book to the side and stood from my bed. Maybe a nice bath would help me forget about the party I was missing out on. I disrobed on my way to the bathroom, rolling my shoulders as I unhooked my bra.

Starting the water, I poured in some bath salts I had bought today on my shopping trip. Usually, I wouldn't waste the money on such needless items, but now that I didn't have to worry about food or housing, I found myself with more money than I was used to in the last few months.

Spending the day outside of the house had been odd. I'd already gotten used to getting up early and working until I passed out at night. At first, I hadn't known what to do with myself. I had climbed into my car and drove around town trying to figure out what to do first.

Then I found the car wash place. I figured I might as well get that done while I made a plan of action. So, while they cleaned my car inside and out, I flipped through my phone checking up on all the things I had missed out on. I made a list of bills that had piled up that needed to be paid as soon as I got my first check. I'd already blown through the last of my money and was desperate to fill it.

My phone had been the only thing I had kept, well, that and my car, since I had given up my apartment. I even had to give up my cat, Marco, named after my cheating ex-boyfriend. I might be able to live in a car but forcing my cat to would have been torture not only for me but the poor beast as well.

When the water filled the tub, I stepped into the steaming liquid and sighed. I piled my hair up on my head in a messy bun and then sank into the water up to my neck. That's the stuff.

This bath salt had been an impulsive purchase while I strolled through the local superstore. That and tampons. I was due for my period any day now. I didn't want to be wearing those things that could double as a diaper while surrounded by so many hot guys.

Thinking of the masters made my mind wander back to the party downstairs. I sadly couldn't hear anything over the music, and I wondered what kind of party it was. A birthday party? A promotion at work? Or maybe it was a fundraiser?

I didn't know why I was bothered by the party at all. I had never been a big socializer, to begin with. Parties were things I flinched at the thought of, let alone going to it. Maybe it was the fact that I knew the men I'd started to see as mine were down there, no doubt being drooled over by some rich and frivolous women. They were all probably batting their eyelashes at them and shoving their fake boobs into their arms.

Snorting, I shifted in the tub. They were probably having the time of their life, Rayne most of all. He seemed to be the type to thrive on the attention, even if he wouldn't give me the time of day. Drake and Allister would let the women come to them. They weren't the type to chase after anyone, well, besides me but that's only because they were messing with me. At least Drake did, I hadn't spent much time with his twin. I was sure there was nothing more to Drake's teasing than just that because he could.

Now, Wynn, I wanted to say he wouldn't even be interested, but I knew a charmer when I saw one. I'd been on the receiving end of his flirting, and it was merciless. The women downstairs, I was assuming there were some unless I had my wires all crossed, wouldn't know what to do with themselves. They were probably arguing over who got to have him first. I chuckled a bit at the thought, and even to my ears, it was bitter.

Stop it, Piper. You're the maid. They're your employers. What did you think would happen?

Forcing the thoughts down, I focused on my little fantasy. Antoine and Marcus with their aloof personalities wouldn't even pay any mind to the women around them.

Antoine might talk to them, but only to the extent of what was polite, never giving them the chance to misunderstand him. Marcus would just glare, his go-to for whenever he caught sight of me, not that he had spoken two words or any words to me for that matter to me. Those hateful eyes would be enough to scare any unwanted attention away.

My line of thoughts made me think about my own dating experiences. It'd been a while since I'd been with anyone. I didn't keep boyfriends for very long. Usually, they thought I was too abrasive to keep around. I didn't pay enough attention to them.

If they were worth paying attention to, then I would. I snorted and rolled my eyes.

I couldn't see myself ever getting bored with any of the Durand brothers. They were all unique in their own way. If anything, I might die of a heart attack from the way they kept surprising me. Those ladies down there didn't know how lucky they were.

Whichever one of the brothers chose them would no doubt take care of them. They'd make sure they didn't leave until they were fully satisfied. A wistful sigh escaped from my lips. Bone liquefying kind of satisfaction. Of course, the masters would send them on their way as soon as they were done, but they would have a happy look on their faces, all too happy to have a one-night stand with them.

I know I would be.

My body warmed at the thought of any of their hands on me. That thought turned into a dark fantasy where I was surrounded by all six brothers, each of them taking their turn to touch and caress me. As my mind wandered so did my hands, cupping my breasts and tweaking my nipples until I gasped. I imagined Wynn's long fingers slipping between my thighs and rubbing circles around my clit.

My breathing came in short pants now as I leaned my head back on the edge of the tub. Drake and Allister would take the fight to my lips, each of them trying to outdo the other, while Rayne would fondle my breasts. Marcus's thick fingers would tease my pussy, only dipping one finger in until I was begging for more.

Antoine, however, would not share me. He would watch from the sidelines, those intense eyes staring at me while his brothers devoured me, watching and waiting his turn until he could have me. His pale eyes would lock with mine as his brothers worked me until I cried out in ecstasy.

When I came down from my self-inflicted high, I felt like a fool. I laughed bitterly as I rubbed a wet hand over my face. What the hell was I thinking? None of them would be with me, let alone share me. I was a lowly maid, nothing more.

I snorted, thinking of what Darren had said. Apparently, I wasn't even trusted to be that either.

Climbing out of the tub, I wrapped a towel around myself. As I pulled on a long t-shirt and boxer shorts I'd stolen from an ex, I heard something from outside my room. Inching my way toward the door, I checked that it was indeed locked.

I moved away from the door but heard it again and more distinctly.

A moan and not just any moan, but a woman's.

An unreasonable amount of anger filled me at the sound of it. I couldn't have them, so they had to rub it in my face? They couldn't take their women to their room and defile them there?

My blood raged in my veins as I ripped the door open. I recognized the broad back pressing a blonde-haired woman against the wall immediately. Drake. Of course, it would be Drake. The smug bastard couldn't leave well enough alone.

Ready to give the man a piece of my mind, I cleared my throat. "Do you mind?"

Slowly, Drake turned from the woman, and I gasped. His eyes practically glowed in the dim hallway and had a sinister hunger in them. Drake licked his lips where a dark liquid covered his chin and lower lip.

My hand came up to my mouth as I stifled a gasp.

Drake let the women in his arms go, and she sagged to the floor, her eyes closed. I didn't have the courage to check if she was still alive as Drake was moving toward me. I scrambled backward and barely got the door closed and locked before he began to bang on it.

"Pretty girl, come out and play," Drake crooned through the wood. When I didn't answer, he banged on the door some more and said sweet nothings to try and get me to open up.

"Don't you want to know what it feels like?"

I shook my head, though he couldn't see it. I pressed my back up against the wood of the door, my legs trembling beneath me.

"I know you do," he purred, his voice reached parts of me that tightened and moistened despite my fear. "I can smell you, you know. Every time you think no one can hear you in the safety of your little room, we can smell your arousal, hear your gasps of pleasure."

My face heated at his words. Could they really? The thought didn't anger me as much as it had when Antoine had made me think they were spying on me.

"Let me in, Piper." He murmured my name like a caress against my skin. "Let me show you just how good it would be."

Moving away from the door for a moment, my hand reached for the doorknob and then another voice joined Drake's.

"What are you doing?"

Antoine.

His voice snapped me out of whatever trance I'd been in, and I jerked my hand away from the door. I backed all the way up until I was on my bed, my eyes never leaving the door. I wrapped my arms around my knees and rocked back and forth as I stared at the door.

"Just having a bit of fun." Drake huffed a laugh.

"Not with her. Get back downstairs and take your... guest with you."

Drake didn't argue, and then after a moment of silence, I thought they had gone. Then Antoine spoke again.

"Are you alright, Miss Billings?"

I didn't answer, too petrified to move let alone speak.

"Piper?" My name in his accented voice shocked me out of my debilitating fear.

Clearing my throat, I blinked. "Yes, I'm fine."

"Good." He paused and then added, "Don't open your door again."

"I won't." I barely got the words out, but there was no answer and no retreating footsteps. I was tempted to check and see if he was gone, but his warning rang clear in my mind.

Lying in bed with the light next to the bed on, my thoughts whirled a mile a minute at what I had seen, not wanting to believe it was true.

It makes sense when I think about it. I glanced down at the book I had been reading. Vampires.

No. No way. I shook my head against the thought. I was just reading too much into it.

Are you though?

The heavy drapes. The barely eating, if at all. I had never seen them eat besides that one cookie with Rayne but that was barely a nibble. Besides that, I'd only ever seen them drink those silver containers which now that I thought of it, that red liquid on Rayne's lips had not been beet juice but blood.

How had I been so stupid? All the signs were there. They didn't come out until night time, well, there was the occasional run-in, but it was always at early morning. Then there were the warnings to not interact with them and to lock my door at night. They had tried to tell me in their own way.

Even Darren trying to get rid of me the first day had been a warning. He had tried to keep me from getting hurt. My heart warmed slightly at the man's unorthodox way of showing he cared. He obviously knew about them. Gretchen probably didn't. She didn't come in often enough, but it would be easy for me to figure it out. I was surprised I hadn't until now.

You were too caught up in your fantasies of them to care.

I scowled at myself for my sex driven brain. I could have easily let myself be eaten by them with all the times I was alone with them, and when I thought about it, I almost had. The incident with Drake came to mind, and I shuddered at how close I'd been to getting bit.

There were no more incidents for the rest of the night. Drake must have given up and gone back to his victim for the night. I worried about the woman and the rest of the guest's downstairs, but my own survival was my primary concern. I was no hero, that was for sure, not that I'd ever claimed to be. The only thing on my mind was getting out of there without getting bit or, worse, killed.

Man, I really had loved this job.

CHAPTER 16

Allister

"WHAT THE FUCK WERE you thinking?" Antoine growled. The sound was low but menacing, and everyone in the room flinched except my brother.

Drake stood before Antoine's desk, his arms crossed over his chest. He didn't even look contrite. No remorse. No guilt. Not that I was surprised. My twin rarely did anything he didn't want to do. He'd never apologized before, and I doubted after all this time he'd do it now.

"I was thinking that I was hungry, and my donor wanted to play." Drake let out gruffly.

With a chuckle, he shrugged. "Who was I to deny her?"

I let out a short laugh, earning me a glare from Antoine. I wasn't the only one laughing either. Wynn smiled. Well, he was always smiling at some stupid shit or another. His own mind made him smile.

Rayne, the little shit, had a perpetual scowl on his lips lately. Something I had a feeling had to do with the pretty maid we're all so preoccupied with.

Speaking of the maid...

Piper Billings. Hard to fucking seduce someone when the legs have been cut out from beneath you. I didn't know what I'd been agreeing to when I'd told Wynn I wouldn't use my powers. Wynn had all the charm of a viper, yes, but take away his fangs and he was still a viper. I couldn't even communicate with the woman.

Maybe I should send her flowers? Women liked flowers, didn't they?

An annoyed groan came from Rayne. "Knock it the fuck off, would you?"

All eyes went to Rayne, pausing Antoine in his interrogation of my brother. Rayne shifted in his seat and frowned. "You all think too loudly."

"I'm sorry if our thoughts are disturbed you." Antoine snapped, not at all sorry. Rayne might have the most annoying gift of all of us. Not only to him, who bitched about it constantly, but to the rest of us. Couldn't have a decent wank without him listening in, let alone a secret.

Pushing up from his seat, Rayne snapped, "I don't see why we all need to be here for this. Drake fucked up. We got it. Good riddance. She was a pest anyway. Get another one. Maybe this time we can find a deaf and mute one. Then all our problems would be solved."

Wynn threw his head back and laughed. "That might help us, but it wouldn't stop you from hearing her thoughts." He paused and stroked his chin. "Wait, does a deaf-mute think in words? Or signs? I'd love to know. Get on that, would you?"

"Fuck you." Rayne flashed his fangs at Wynn, making Marcus tense beside Antoine.

"Enough, both of you." Antoine steepled his fingers and leaned back in his chair. "We want the maid we have, so no more talk of getting another one. You lot just need to keep your fangs and your cocks where they belong." Antoine's eyes slid back around the room and landed on Drake. "I don't want to see another incident like last night's, and if I find any of you doing what this arrogant piece of shit has done, I'll send you to our sire. See how you like a century or two under his thumb."

The room went still. None of us wanted to go to our sire's home. The Russian fucker was worse than Antoine and crazier too. At least, Antoine we could trust not to stake us in our sleep because we'd annoyed him. Our sire wouldn't be so lenient.

"I'm sorry." Drake ducked his head. "I won't do it again."

Antoine's eyes shifted to Rayne. The redhead shook his head, his shaggy hair jerking side to side with his head. "Good. Then I believe this meeting is over." He raised a hand to Marcus. "Lock the front door and keep an eye out for our skittish maid. She is no doubt packing her bags right this very second."

Antoine stood, adjusting his suit jacket. "The rest of you go to bed while I clean up our brother's mess."

We filed out of the room, our heads hung low, thoroughly chastised. I followed my twin on his way to his room. Drake tried to shut his door behind him, but I grabbed a hold of it and pushed my way in.

"You really fucked up this time." I threw myself down in his arm chair, folding my hands over my stomach. "What did you expect to gain from your little display? Did you think she would come out of her room with open veins?"

"More like legs," Drake snorted, pulling his shirt over his head.

We both had the same tattoo across our left breast. The symbol of our house, the

Durand black crow with the words *Sanguinem meum in saecula* wrapped around it. It loosely translated to 'Blood of my blood, now and forever.' A bit of irony there as our house sigil was a bad omen, but it was the only thing that has kept us alive over the years. And we had Antoine to thank for that.

"At least I'm actually trying to do something." Drake kicked his shoes off and pulled on a new shirt. "You have your thumb so far up your ass trying to find some fancy way around Wynn's rules."

I frowned, not getting what he was saying.

Drake chuckled. "Do you really think Wynn is playing by the rules?"

Sighing, I kicked my feet out in front of me. "I guess you have a point there. So, what do I do? Corner her and charm her out of her panties? The same ones that are so wet for Wynn?"

"No, you pull her out from under him mid-fuck." Drake shook his head, scoffing. "Seriously, some days I wonder how we ever shared the same womb."

Ignoring his jab, I stood. "I ask the same thing, asshole."

I walked to his bedroom door, pulling it open. Before going out, I turned back to him. "If you were in my position, what would you do? To charm her?"

Drake glanced over at me and then smirked. "I'd whisper sweet nothings in her ears until she didn't know who or what she wanted anymore. Until all she thought about was you."

CHAPTER 17

Piper

I DIDN'T GET A wink of sleep that night. As soon as I got my wits about me, I packed my bag and waited until dawn. If they were vampires, they wouldn't be able to go outside in the sunlight. Also, previous experience told me they wouldn't be up this early anyway.

I grabbed my bag and moved at a snail's pace toward the bedroom door. I hesitated before I flicked the lock and opened the door without warning. No one was waiting outside my door, but that didn't make me relax. As far as I knew, someone was waiting to jump me at the front door.

Stepping out into the hallway, my eyes flickered to the spot I'd seen Drake biting that woman before. However, there was no sign that it ever happened. No blood, nobody. Just the empty hallway.

Part of me wanted to believe that I had imagined it. That it was all a bad dream, but deep down inside of me, I knew it hadn't been. I was stupid to even think it might be some morbid fantasy conjured up by the book I'd been reading.

A smart person would have gone out the back, but my car was still parked in the front. If I went through the back, I'd risk the chance of running into Gretchen or Darren who were no doubt in the kitchen right now. I didn't want Gretchen to know anything was wrong, and Darren would figure it out right away and might tell Antoine. I couldn't risk it.

I winced at every creak the floor made as I made my way through the hallways and down the staircase. The bottom floor was still a mess from the party the night before. Glasses and plates sat on side tables. Clothing had been discarded without care at the foot of the steps.

My nose crinkled. Someone had been in a hurry.

Part of me was thankful that I was leaving. The mess would probably be on my list of chores to clean up today, but I'd left my room before they could leave me my little note. I so didn't want to deal with the leftovers from last night.

Just thinking about seeing whoever they had taken to bed with them the night before made my heart clench strangely. I'd understand if it had only been Wynn I'd been thinking about, but even Antoine and Rayne came to mind.

Shaking my head, I chastised myself for letting myself care about those monsters.

Almost home free, my shoulders relaxed as my hand touched the doorknob. I began to turn it only to find that it wouldn't move. I twisted it and jerked on the knob but nothing. I tried to unlock it, but there was a bolt I'd never noticed before that required a key.

Fuck.

My heart beat rapidly in my chest, and I realized I had to go through the back. I didn't have a choice.

However, before I could head that way, a voice stopped me. Frozen to the spot, I wanted to pretend like I hadn't heard Antoine calling my name. What was he even doing up this early? Every inch of me wanted to run, to scream for help, but I knew no one there would help me. I was on my own.

"Don't make me ask twice, Piper." Antoine's warning tone told me I better come to him, or I wouldn't like the outcome. Maybe if I pretended that I hadn't seen anything last night, he'd let me go. Just heading off to take care of somethings on my day off.

Sitting my bag down on the ground, I turned around and made my way to where Antoine sat in the living room. My eyes locked onto where he lounged on the couch, completely at ease. On the coffee table in front of him was a piece of the vase I had broken on the first day.

I stopped at the edge of the couch not moving any further, my eyes flickering between him and the ceramic. "What can I help you with, Master Durand?" I decided to pretend like I didn't know anything about last night, about what they were. No need to let him in on it if he didn't know.

Antoine smiled slightly, no hint of the fangs I now knew were beneath those gorgeous lips. "Now, let's not pretend here. I have far too much respect for you to do that." He gestured to the chair across from him. "Please, have a seat."

I glanced down at the seat and then back to Antoine. "I think I'll stand."

The smile on his face wilted slightly. "Very well." He shifted in his seat and adjusted his suit jacket, his pale hair falling over his shoulders making him look even more sinister. "It seems one of my brothers has let our little secret slip. Now, you understand that I can't just let you leave knowing what you know."

My heart jumped at the implications of his words and my lower lip trembled. I slapped my hand over my mouth, not wanting to give away my fear. It was no idle threat. Just me knowing what they were made me a threat to their very being. I'd be disappointed if he didn't want to kill me. It would make things kind of melodramatic if he just let me leave.

"Now, get that look off your face, I'm not going to kill you." Antoine leaned back, throwing one arm over the back of the couch and crossing one leg over the other.

I squinted at him. "You're not?"

"No," Antoine answered simply and then sighed, rubbing his forehead with his forefingers. "You have to understand our situation here, Miss Billings."

"Oh, I understand perfectly." I snorted and crossed my arms over my chest as I rocked back on my heels. "You are a bunch of blood-sucking fiends that use your looks to get what you want." Now that I had opened my mouth, I couldn't seem to stop the outpour. "How many people have you killed? How many maids? Is that why you needed a new one?" I scoffed and wagged my finger at him. "I will *not* be the next one on your list of victims. I'd sooner snort garlic."

Antoine stared at me calmly. "Are you quite finished?"

A bit taken back by his words, I paused and then nodded. "Yes, I suppose I am."

"Good, now to answer your questions, zero is the number of people we have killed," he began. "Unlike those ridiculous movies you humans are determined to burn your brains out with, we vampires need blood to survive, but we don't drink until death. Our stomachs couldn't handle that much in any case, and for another, if we killed everyone we bit, then we wouldn't be able to stay under the radar.

"For your second question, no, we haven't eaten our previous maids. The reason we have gone through so many is that each and every one of them couldn't keep their noses in their own business or were so enamored by my brothers that they would sneak into their beds. It really became quite a problem. My brothers would fight over them, and all sorts of chaos would be unleashed."

I could totally see that. The brothers were something to behold. If I didn't need the job so bad, I would have jumped on them the moment I could. Thinking about it now, it seemed my money troubles were the least of my worries. Not getting eaten was pretty high on the list now.

Antoine pursed his lips in thought. "You, however, have yet to cause any fighting." I frowned a bit disappointed in my lack of sexual prowess. "Do not be mistaken. All of us are quite taken by you, Miss Billings." He paused, and his eyes bored into me as he purred my name. "Piper."

That word wiggled through my ears, through my veins, and settled deep between my legs. I pressed them together tightly and forced back my reaction to him and his words. Fucking hormones.

"I have to say you are the most frustrating human I've ever had the pleasure of having in my household, and I've had quite a lot over the last few hundreds of years."

I gaped at the admittance.

"Don't look so surprised." Antoine lifted his chin, an arrogant sneer on his face. "Looks can be deceiving, especially when vampires are involved."

He'd said it. He'd actually called themselves vampires.

"What else is true then?" I couldn't help but ask. "Do you have a reflection?"

Antoine's eyes glittered with amusement. "Of course. Hard to shave without one."

My confidence built as I realized he was going to answer my questions. "What about garlic? Beheading? Stakes through the heart?"

Clucking his tongue, Antoine cocked his head to the side. "Are you looking to kill me, Piper?"

"Don't say my name like that," I snapped back, shifting from one foot to the other. For some reason, just hearing my name on his lips unsettled me, made my guard slip, just a little.

"Why?" Antoine flashed a fanged grin. "That is your name, is it not?"

I licked my lips and swallowed, nodding.

"Don't you like it?" Antoine's eyes bore into me. "You could be very happy here, Piper, if you just let go of your prejudices and allow us the same rights as you give other humans."

Scoffing, I let out a nervous laugh.

"Something funny?"

Shaking my head, I rubbed my arm, trying to remove the goosebumps that had appeared. "You obviously don't know me well enough if you think I rate humans very high on the list. They're just as bad as you."

"I see." He peered at me beneath those pale lashes, trying to figure me out. "And will you stake me in my sleep?"

"Not if you let me go."

He slid a hand through his hair and gave me a knowing smirk. "And where would you go? Back to living in your car?"

"It's not that bad," I admitted, dropping my eyes to the oriental rug.

"You don't really want to go now, do you, Piper?" Antoine stood from the couch and moved closer to me. "Not when you have a debt to pay."

I knew he was taunting me with the broken vase, but I didn't take the bait. I stared up at him, my mouth going dry. I shook my head, unable to come up with an answer.

"I didn't think so." Antoine cupped my face with his hand and leaned down until his lips brushed mine. When he pulled back, his face had returned to his usual superior smirk. "Now, take your bag back to your room and clean this place up. It's a pig sty."

Gaping at what had just happened, I didn't have a chance to argue before Antoine had disappeared to God knew where. As I took my bag back to my room, I thought about why I was staying. Was I really that hung up on these guys that I would risk my life to stay here?

If I were truthful with myself, that would be a resounding yes. However, I wasn't that self-aware. I told myself it was to keep an eye on them. If I knew their secret, then they would be held accountable at least by someone.

Dropping my bag on the floor, I changed into my work clothes. I didn't know what the future held for me if I ever became useless to them. Most likely, I'd be turned into one of their meals. What I did know was that I couldn't leave them, not just because of what Antoine said. I did owe them, but I wouldn't just roll over to save my own ass.

If I left, they would get a new maid, and that one might not be as smart as me. Also, the thought of another woman being around the masters made my skin crawl. I still hadn't come to terms with my feelings for them, especially now that I knew what they were.

I couldn't let anyone else get hurt. At least, if I were here, I'd be able to keep them in line. Maybe save a few lives and hopefully not lose my own in the process. So much for not being a hero. I was gunning for the spot of the dumbest one of the year.

CHAPTER 18

Piper

HALFWAY THROUGH CLEANING UP the mess from last night I remembered it was supposed to be my day off. However, I shrugged and finished it anyway.

I needed the distraction.

Who could blame me, really? I was working in a household of six gorgeous men, and they were all vampires. To say my brain wasn't nearly fried from the very concept of it all would be putting it lightly.

"You're staying?" Darren asked.

I paused where I was cleaning up the living room to look at him. He stood with his back straight by the front door, too suave to lean like us normal people. The surprise on his face didn't bother me. If I had been in his position, I probably wouldn't think I would stay. Hell, I wasn't even sure if I had come to terms with it yet myself.

Lifting a shoulder like it was no big deal, I sighed. "What can I say? I need the job."

"But you know what they are..." He trailed off, moving into the living room. He picked up a lamp that had been knocked over. "Why would you want to stay?"

"Why do you?" I shot back.

Taking the trash bag from me so we could work together, his next words surprised me. "I owe them a life debt. I couldn't leave even if I wanted to."

"Really?" I arched a brow, throwing a few more plastic cups into the bag. Was it a kegger or an elegant party? It seemed like a bit of both from what I was picking up. "How did they warrant such a debt? Did you break an expensive vase too?"

We shared a chuckle.

"No, they saved me from the streets."

"Oh."

"Don't look at me like that. No pity here." Darren picked up the cleaning spray and began to clean the mirrors. "My mother was a drug addict and didn't ever give two craps about me."

"And your dad?"

He rubbed the mirror a bit more vigorously. "I never met him. I was begging on the street from the time I was three. Eventually, my mother died from an overdose and left me alone to fend for myself, not that it changed much. Just that instead of begging, I started to get involved with the wrong kind of business."

I cocked my head to the side wondering what he meant. Prostitution? Drug dealing? I didn't ask, not wanting to stop this sudden flood of information he was giving me. He'd tell me when he was ready.

"That's when Antoine found me." He paused and twisted part way to look at me. "I was only ten. I shouldn't have been in the alleyway that late at night anyway. It was only asking for trouble." He huffed a laugh. "But I thought I was tough. Had a pocket knife and a chip on my shoulder. But all that gets you in this world is dead."

The darkness in his eyes made me sad. This man, who was more polished and sophisticated than anyone I'd ever met, had lived through such a traumatizing childhood only to end up here? He was so much stronger than anyone I'd ever met.

"They're not as bad as they come off," Darren started again, turning back to the mirror. "They may be different than us, but they're no more different than the humans around us. Believe me when I say even humans can be monsters."

I nodded. I understood that. There were worse things than people who happened to need a bit of blood to survive.

"How long have you been working here?" I picked up the broom and swept it across the floor, focusing on picking up the shards of glass that had broken off from the knocked-over lamp.

"A hundred and twelve."

My head jerked up so fast, the broom knocked into a side table. "Wait, what?"

Darren's eyes crinkled at the sides. "You heard me right. This year will be one hundred and twelve years of employment."

I stared at him for a moment, my eyes searching his face for those years he claimed to have served. Unless he colored his hair, there wasn't a hint of gray in his dark locks. His skin was smooth and unblemished. He couldn't be older than thirty if that.

"How?" I stuttered, moving closer to him.

His lips curled up his eyes squinting with his smile. "I owe them a life debt. I can't very well complete it the way I was, sickly and underfed. Master Durand made sure I would be able to serve them until I was no longer needed."

"But you're not like them. Not a vampire." I breathed the word like it was a secret.

"No. I'm not."

He was being evasive. That I could understand. If the vampires could make a human live longer without the handicap of drinking blood or weakness of the sun, humans would kill for it. They would hunt them down and demand them to change them. Sure, some would pay for it or even try to seduce their way into their good graces, but even so, the masters wouldn't want that to happen.

"Will they do that to me?" I blinked, staring down at the ground. My heartbeat quickened. I wasn't sure I wanted to live forever.

Darren's laughter startled me. My eyes jumped from the ground. Darren's head fell back as he laughed a great big belly laugh. He laughed so long that it started to irritate me.

"It's not that funny," I muttered, turning back to my sweeping.

Coughing and then clearing his throat, Darren walked over to my side, placing a hand on my shoulder. "My apologies. It will take more than a broken vase to gain eternal life." He winked at me and then patted me on the shoulder. "Then again with your track record, you may need it to pay back what you've broken."

I chuckled and shook my head, shoving him on the shoulder. "Jerk."

"Alright, back to work." He waved a hand around the still disarrayed room. "Then get some sleep. I'm sure you were tossing and turning all night." I tried to deny it, but he gave me a knowing look. "I didn't sleep for a week after I found out what Master Durand was." He barked a laugh. "That also might have been the fever I was recovering from though. Hard to tell."

I snorted and rolled my eyes.

We continued to clean until the room was spotless and then we moved onto the dining room. It was just as bad in there if not worse. I grimaced as I picked up a pair of lady's panties by the end of my broomstick.

"What was the theme of this party?" I stuck my tongue out and shuddered. "Who could lose the most clothes?"

Darren sniffed. "The masters have some over-enthusiastic guests."

"You're telling me," I grumbled and then I remembered Drake and then moaning woman in the hallway. "Why isn't there any blood?"

"Blood?"

"Yes." I leaned over the table and scooped several plates and cups into the trash bags. "You know, vampires drink blood." When he only stared at me, I reached up to my face and put my fingers in my mouth like I had two long fangs. "With fangs?"

"I know what you mean, you daft girl."

I went back to filling the bag with trash. "Then where's the blood? I've found trash, panties, and all manner of other things, worse than a fucking frat house if you ask me, but no blood. Why is that?"

"We're neat eaters," Wynn answered, causing Darren and I to freeze. He moved around the table, his eyes locked onto me. Those piercing blue eyes were more dangerous and tempting than they had been over eight hours ago. When he stopped on the other side of the chair from me, my fingers curled tightly around the trash bag. "Are you afraid of me now, Piper?"

I licked my lips, my eyes darting down and then back up to his face. "I... I don't know. Are you going to bite me?"

Wynn's lips curled back, far enough that his canines protruded over his mouth. "Not unless you're offering, love. Are you?"

I shook my head profusely. "No."

"Then no." He closed his mouth and cocked his head to the side. "I won't bite you, and neither will any of my brothers."

I opened my mouth to argue that Drake had seemed more than happy to take me whether or not he had my permission, but as if he were reading my mind, Wynn added, "No matter how much they tease and torment you about it."

Chancing a look at Darren, who was just barely holding back his laughter, I muttered,

"Good to know I amuse you all so much. Fucking bastards."

"Now, is that any way to talk about your master?" Wynn slipped around the chair and leaned against the table's edge, caging me in.

"Pfft. Master. You're no more my master than you are as charming as you think you are." I jerked my head in his direction, then continued to clean off the table. "Now, if you don't mind, I have work to do and a nap to take."

Wynn lifted his hands up, his lips pressing into a thin line. "Far be it from me to keep a lady from her sleep." He glanced over to Darren. "I'll be heading down now. Make sure we don't lose our maid again."

Darren smirked at me, placing a hand over his chest and inclining his head. "Of course, Master."

My eyes followed Wynn out of the corner of my eye until he was had disappeared down the hallway and not back upstairs. "Where's he going?"

"To the basement, where all the masters' sleep during the day."

I gathered up the final bag of trash and followed Darren into the kitchen. "In coffins?"

"Why would they do that?" Darren arched a brow as he dumped the dishes into the sink. Rolling up his sleeves, he turned on the water and begun to wash them.

I took up the place beside him and rinsed them before putting them into the drainer. "They always do in the movies and books."

Darren stopped washing for a moment to stare at me. "Do you think that everything you see or read is right? That perhaps those things were leaked, purposely placed there by those who do not wish their secrets revealed?"

I hummed. He continued washing. We stood there in silence for a few moments, and then I asked, "Does Gretchen know?"

Giving me a sideways look, Darren handed me a plate. "Who do you think fills the silver containers in the refrigerator?" He took the cup I had been rinsing and gestured with his head. "Why don't you go lay down, and we can talk more about it later? A lot has happened in a short period of time."

I didn't argue. My eyes burned, and my head ached from all the new information. I simply turned away from and walked up the stairs. I didn't stop walking until I was inside my room. I stripped down to my underwear, not bothering to put on a tank top or sleep shirt and collapsed on top of the covers of my bed. I was out before my head ever hit the pillow.

CHAPTER 19

Piper

BLOOD. THE SHARP TANG of it filled every orifice of my being. I stood in the dining room once more the trash bag in my hand but alone. Those cups I'd picked up weren't filled with the residue of the alcohol they'd been drinking but instead were overflowing with syrupy dark red liquid.

I glanced down at my hands and gasped, dropping the trash bag. My palms were coated red and shined from the freshly spilled blood. My pulse pounded in my ears, and I tried to rub it off on my pants, but it wouldn't come off.

Spinning on my heel, I raced to the kitchen. At the sink, I flicked on the sink. Putting my hands beneath the scalding water, I rubbed at my hands until they were raw, but still, it wouldn't come off. I cried and yelled out. I kicked the lower cabinets and sunk to the ground, burying my face in my arms and knees.

"Why, Miss Billings?" Antoine's accented voice purred, and my head peeked up. "Why are you crying?"

Letting out little gasping sobs, I held my hands out. "I can't get it off. No matter how much I scrub it won't come off."

Antoine knelt at my side, his pale hair falling over his shoulder and he bent his head over my hands. "I see," he mused and then smirked at me, a hint of a fang showing. "I think I can take care of that."

Without warning, his tongue darted out and lapped at my hands. The warm wet muscle stroked along my palms in a strange but somehow erotic manner. I squirmed in place but didn't take my hands away from him. For some reason, under Antoine's attention, the blood was coming off where the soap and water had done nothing.

When he pulled one of my fingers into his mouth, my lips formed an o-shape. My thighs rubbed together, and I begged the aching need forming there to dissipate. Antoine's nostrils flared, and his eyes flashed up to meet mine, a low growl coming from his throat as he moved in closer.

"Don't be so greedy, brother," Wynn appeared at my other side, taking my other hand from his brother. His pouty lips parted, and his tongue darted out, trailing a line from my hands to my elbow. He seemed to care more about tasting every inch of my skin than the actual blood on it.

I sighed and wiggled a bit closer to Wynn. I wanted his mouth on me, those lips pulling on flesh far lower and aching with each touch of their ministrations.

Another low growl pulled my attention from the dark-haired Adonis to Rayne, who jumped over the island and landed before me. His ember eyes flashed red as he prowled up to me, his fingers closing in around my ankles, pulling my legs down and apart. His head dipped, and his eyes closed as he inhaled.

"Now that's what I call a wet dream."

My eyes blinked at him, and my head cocked to the side. "What?"

The scene blurred around me, and my lashes fluttered open. A part of me sank at the realization that Antoine and Wynn weren't really there. That part was quickly replaced with relief at the absence of blood covering my hands and arms where I laid on my bed.

I let out a heavy breath. Well, it didn't take a genius to figure out what that dream had been all about. Vampires and hot men. Double trouble. A shiver of desire rippled through me, and I realized the need in my dream had passed over to the real world.

What was it that Rayne had said? I giggled a bit, shifting to my side to face the wall. Wet dream indeed.

Checking the time on the clock by the bed, I figured I had a bit more time before I needed to hunt down something to eat. I allowed my eyes to flutter shut once more, hoping to recapture the image of the three of them coming onto me all at once. Sure, Rayne was an ass, but a hot ass. And it's my dream! He doesn't need to know what I flick my bean to.

With a secretive smile, I slid my hand beneath the covers and dipped them between my legs, letting out a ragging groan as my fingers found my clit.

"Would you like a hand with that?"

My fingers stilled at the sound of Rayne's voice, my eyes shooting open. I sat up, utter mortification engulfing my very being. The bed shifted, and I twisted around to see Rayne's amber eyes inches from my face.

"What are you doing in here?"

Rayne's lopsided grin made my clit pulse, and I scowled to myself. Down, girl.

"It's not my fault you don't know how to lock your door." Tipping his head to the side, his red hair fell over his eyes, his nose brushing along the curse of my neck. "I was walking back to my room and could hardly resist those sweet, needy whimpers you were making."

"I was not," I pushed him back with a glare, "and that still doesn't give you a right to come into my room without permission."

"Actually, it does." Rayne smirked at my confusion. "I'm your boss. I can go and do whatever I want. That includes..." He looped his fingers around the strap of my tank top and pulled it down over my shoulder. "...you, and now that you're staying, we'll have plenty of time to get acquainted."

What the fuck was wrong with this kid? Did turning into a vampire make him lose all his sense of decency? I wasn't some piece of meat he could take a bite out of any time that he wanted.

You weren't singing that tune just a few moments ago, now were you?

Shut up. Dream Rayne and real-life Rayne are two totally different creatures.

My hand lashed out on its own. My fist collided with the side of Rayne's face. The pain was sharp and explosive. I gasped and jerked my hand back, glaring at him and his stupid face.

"Did you just punch me?" Rayne gaped, his face hadn't even moved when my fist crumbled against his face. "I can't believe you just hit me."

"You!" I shouted, jumping from the bed. "You broke my hand." I held my injured hand out for him to see and then grimaced, holding it close to my body.

Rayne scoffed, waving me off. "You should have thought about that before you decided to punch a vampire."

"Just because you suck blood and have granite for skin doesn't mean you can harass me whenever you want."

"Oh, come on, don't act like you didn't want me to." He leered at me, and I had the urge to hit him again, even with my broken hand.

"What's going on here?"

Both our heads jerked to the door where Wynn stood in all his gloriously delicious self. His flexing biceps shifted beneath his button-down black shirt. He had braided his long black hair, and it hung over his shoulder, making him look even more the forbidden temptation.

"She hit me." Rayne pointed an accusing finger at my fist with a sneer.

Wynn didn't even spare his brother a glance, his blue eyes immediately going to my hand where I clutched it to my chest. "You're hurt."

He stepped quickly across the room until he stood before me. With compassion in his eyes, Wynn reached out and cupped my hand. I inhaled sharply and clenched my teeth. His fingers stroked my skin where it had already begun to turn purple and blue.

"Rayne."

The single word made the redhead rush to Wynn's side. Rayne's mouth barely opened to spout whatever excuse he had before Wynn's spare hand whipped out and hit him across the face. The sudden impact sent Rayne flying into the wall, knocking over my side table and the lamp that went with it in the process. The sound of glass breaking made me wince, and my head turned away from Wynn to where Rayne crouched on the ground.

His amber eyes flashed red, but unlike in my dream, they weren't full of lust but anger. His eyes locked onto me as he swiped his thumb against the side of his mouth, coming away red. I swallowed hard. I was going to pay for that later.

"Come, let's get your hand taken care of." Wynn wrapped an arm around my shoulders and turned me away from Rayne, leading me out of my room. Over his shoulder, Wynn told Rayne, "Clean that up and then make yourself scarce before I tell Antoine what you've done."

I could feel Rayne's eyes boring into my back as we left, and I turned my head to Wynn. "Thank you. I'm sorry to be such a bother."

"Nonsense. Rayne has a big mouth and has years to go before he will fully mature. We hope." He winked, and I giggled despite my pain.

"I have to say, even though he deserved it, I am regretting hitting him." I flexed my wrist and hissed. "I didn't know vampires were so... hard." I flushed at my wording and flicked my gaze over at Wynn, but if he had noticed my slip up, he didn't show it.

"There are many things about us you will have to learn if you are going to continue working here," he mused, leading me down the hallway.

I realized after a moment that we weren't going to the kitchen but only gave it a brief thought before asking, "And what else should I know?"

Pushing the door open to his bedroom, he flashed me a fanged grin. "You will have to learn for yourself."

I hesitated at his doorway, my mouth falling open slightly. Did he really want me to go into his room?

Wynn urged me forward with a reassuring nod.

Taking a deep breath, I took the final step into his room. Dark oaks decorated his furniture, from the tall armoire standing on one end of the room to the four-poster bed with its wine-colored sheets. I'd been in his room many times, getting his laundry and putting it back. However, I never had to make his bed. Any of theirs. I honestly didn't know what they had me around for other than to clean their clothes and pick up after their parties.

"Do you not sleep in your bed?" I spun around and covered my mouth, my eyes widening. "I'm sorry. That's not any of my business."

Wynn's lips curled up slightly, his head dipping as moved in closer. "No, it's alright. It's not surprising you noticed we don't exactly keep the same hours as you."

"Yeah." I let out a nervous giggle. "The days are pretty quiet with only Darren for company. He's not exactly the talkative type."

"My apologies." He moved into his bathroom for a moment and then came back out with a first aid kit.

Gesturing for me to take a seat on the edge of his bed, I hesitated again. It was bad enough to be in Wynn's room but to sit on his bed? Get a grip. It's not like he's going to ravish you right there with the bedroom door open.

The mattress sank beneath me and the sudden urge to lay back on it was almost too much to ignore. Man, I thought my bed was soft. What a waste.

"What is it?"

My eyes jerked up from the bed to see Wynn watching me with a bemused look. I blinked rapidly, stumbling over my words as my face heated. "I was just thinking what a pity it is to have such a soft bed but not getting to use it."

Taking my hand in his, Wynn opened the first aid kit. "I understand how you would see it that way, but believe me, it gets plenty of action."

I flushed even hotter at his words, forcing myself not to picture the things he could be doing in the bed beneath us. What he could be doing in it to me. Turning my eyes away from the bed, I watched Wynn pick through the first aid kit. He pulled out a large wrap and a tiny vial of dark liquid rolled against the side of the box.

"What's that?" I pointed at the vial.

Wynn picked it up and held it up between his thumb and forefinger. "This is my blood."

My brows furrowed. "Why do you have a vial of your blood in there?"

Shrugging a shoulder, he rolled the vial around on his hand. "We all do. For emergencies."

"What kind of emergencies?"

Wynn sat the wrap back in the box and moved closer to me so I could get a better look. "Well, for instance. Your hand is very much broken. At least a few fingers. You'll need to get a cast on it. However," he held the bottle out to me, "if you drank this, your hand would be healed in a matter of minutes."

Astonishment filled my chest, and I stared far too long at the vial before turning to him. "What's the catch?"

Wynn grinned, wrapping his fingers around the vial and successfully hiding it from my view. "I knew I liked you."

Ignoring the flutter in my chest at his words, I turned in place to show him I wasn't going to give up my questioning.

"If you drank this, it would heal your hand certainly." His eyes dipped down to where my hand sat between us, his fingers trailing along the skin ever so slightly. It didn't exactly hurt, but it made my flesh feel hot and achy. "But then it would also give you a slight immunity to my... charms." He grinned, his eyes peering up at me from beneath his lashes. "As well as other side effects."

"Like? And is that immunity to just you or all vampires?"

"Well, aren't you a needy one?"

God, he had no idea. Still, I kept my mouth shut eager to hear what he had to say. If his blood would make me immune to all the others' charms as he said, I would down it regardless of any other side effects. I was already at a disadvantage, being one of the only women surrounded by all this raging testosterone. Now that I knew they were vampires, I was even more vulnerable to their whims as Rayne had almost shown me.

"Sadly, no." Wynn's lips pursed together. "Only me and the side effects, while not unpleasant, might not be something you want to deal with."

"But it'll heal my hand?" My eyebrows rose up in question. I didn't exactly have health care or dental for that matter. I couldn't afford a trip to the ER to fix my hand. If I could fix it for free and with little to no side effects, then I'd take it.

"Yes." Wynn watched me curiously and then opened his hand offering me the vial. "Do you want it?"

I licked my dry lips, my eyes moving from the vial to Wynn's eyes and back again. "Would you think badly if I did?"

"Of course not." Wynn frowned. "I would have offered it right away had I thought you wouldn't be disgusted by it."

Now it was my turn to frown. "Why would you think that?"

"Well, it's blood. My blood. You'd have to drink it," he explained as if it were obvious. "Most would run screaming from the room or at least curse me for even suggesting it."

I snorted. "I'm still here, aren't I? If you're being a vampire hasn't sent me packing yet, then I don't think a little blood will." I didn't mention the fact that I already had tried to leave once, but since he didn't bring it up, I figured Antoine had kept it quiet.

"Besides," I sighed, "I'd rather not have to deal with a cast. It's hard enough cleaning up after you all with two hands let alone one."

"True enough." Wynn nodded once and held the vial out to me. "Here."

Taking the vial from him, I popped the cap and stared at it for a moment before giving Wynn a weak smile. "Salut."

CHAPTER 20

Wynn

ANTOINE WAS GOING TO kill me. Why had I given Piper my blood? I was already attracted to her, I didn't need another reason to want to be near her.

Maybe you wanted to make sure you won.

So maybe not being able to use my powers was a bit irritating, but was I really so unsure of my own abilities that I had to make her want me?

The moment my blood hit her mouth, I wanted to reach for her. I wanted to show her that all the things she dreamed about could come true. I heard the way she touched herself in her room, we all did. She wasn't exactly quiet, though I was sure she didn't feel that way. In fact, if Piper knew how we all stared at the ceiling of our daytime resting place, she'd run away and never come back.

Women were strange that way. After all these years, I still hadn't completely wrapped my head around their actions. Whether it be France or the U.S., the actions of women astounded me.

Like the way that Piper drank the vial of my blood without a hint of revulsion. Most women would have been disgusted by the thought. However, she also hadn't quite reacted the way we had thought when she found out we were vampires.

There had been no attacking or threatening us. Piper had tried to leave, but a simple word or two from Antoine was all it took to convince her to stay. One could chalk that up to Antoine's persuasive abilities, but it didn't keep her from still interacting with us.

When I'd seen her in the dining room afterward, she hadn't seemed afraid. In fact, if anything, she had grown even more of a backbone, as if us being monsters somehow gave her even more reason to speak out against us.

I chuckled at that thought.

"What's so funny?" Piper asked, her brows crinkling. "Did I do it wrong? Was I supposed to sip it?"

Shaking my head, I touched her hand, making her eyes drop to it. "No, that was fine. Don't mind me, my mind got away from me for a moment. How's your hand?" I stroked the line of her knuckles which had been purple and blue before, but now it was more of a sickly yellow.

Piper frowned and wiggled her fingers. "It's healing, I think? I doesn't hurt like before. It only aches some."

"Good." I bobbed my head, patting her arm before standing. I needed to put some distance between us before the blood in her took full effect. "Then you should be completely healed within the hour."

"Really?"

The shock in her voice made me smile. "Would I lie to you?"

Piper seemed to think about it for a moment, her head cocked to the side. "I'm not sure. I don't really know you all that well. So, you might be lying to me right this moment and I'll be a vampire by morning."

I snorted, barking out a laugh. "That is truer than you know but becoming one of us takes far more than a little vial of my blood."

"Is that so?" The way her lips parted with an eagerness to learn made me want to teach her everything else I knew of being a vampire, including the more salacious aspects that only could be taught without clothing.

Turning my back on her so as not to jump her on the spot, I strode to the bathroom and replaced the first aid kit. "You should keep that wrap on your hand, at least for appearances sake. Rayne would run and tattle the moment he found out I gave you my blood."

"Is that wrong?" Her voice closer than it had been before.

As I turned around to face her in the doorway of the bathroom, I was surprised she had snuck up on me so easily. Obviously, my mind was elsewhere, or that was what I told myself.

Offering her a small smile, I kept my distance though every part of me screamed to take her. "It's frowned upon." Her pouty lips turned down in a frown and I was quick to add, "Don't worry about it. If anyone gets in trouble, it will be me."

She seemed to think about it for a moment but then gave a curt nod. "Alright. Well, I should probably get going before someone sees me in here."

"Why?" The word escaped my mouth before my brain even processed it. Piper stopped in the doorway and turned back to me an adorable confusion on her face. "I mean, why would anyone care you are in here? You're the maid after all. Maybe you needed to clean up a spill. I can be awfully clumsy."

She smiled, and if my heart still beat, it would have skipped one.

"I don't see any mess."

I grabbed the cup off my sink, filled it with water, and then promptly dumped it on the ground. "There. Now you have an excuse."

Piper giggled. The sound of it was like peals of angels coming from Aphrodite's lips. I wanted her to do it again.

"Why did you become a maid?" I asked, leaning back against the sink. "You are far too pretty to be cleaning toilets."

Piper's laughter cut off. Her eyes dimmed and her mouth pressed into a thin line. Instead of answering me, she moved further into my bathroom which made the large room feel small with her presence. Piper's scent filled my senses the closer she came, and I almost reached out despite myself, but she completely bypassed me. She grabbed a towel from the cabinet and knelt on the floor, wiping up the water.

"Piper?" I didn't like the silence that had come from my question. "I apologize if I have offended you, I didn't mean—"

"You didn't." She shook her head, standing with the towel. "Offend me that is. I just don't want you to think badly of me."

"You don't?" I arched a brow at her, making her flush. Happy that she was no longer frowning, I stepped into her space ignoring the warning in me telling me to keep my distance. "I don't think I could think badly of you, no matter what you have done in the past."

She let out a little nervous laugh, tucking her hair behind her ear. "I wouldn't bet on it."

I smiled down at her. "You punched a vampire and lived. You didn't go screaming into the night when you found out what we were. Believe me, there isn't much that surprises me, but you have, Piper Billings."

That beautiful shade of red on her cheeks spread to her neck and chest. I wanted to see how far down it went but curled my fingers into fists to keep myself from finding out.

"More from my own stupidity than bravery," she belittled herself, shifting in place, her eyes not meeting mine. Piper was quiet for a moment before holding up the towel. "I better put this in the laundry."

She scurried out of the bathroom, not answering my question. I followed after her, watching her every movement as she practically ran for the door. Before she darted out of it, she did stop and turn back to me.

"Thank you, Master Durand." She held her hand up with a small polite smile. "For healing me."

She ducked out of the room before I could correct her.

"... Call me Wynn..."

CHAPTER 21

Piper

I HAD TO ADMIT I expected more to happen after I drank the vial of Wynn's blood, but there I was, putting away books in the library later that evening, hand healed and nothing else.

Turning my hand this way and that, I muttered to myself, "You'd think I'd at least get super strength or heightened senses from drinking vampire blood."

With my arms full of books, I made my way over to the shelves. Someone had been binge reading and leaving them out for me to put up, out of character for the usually neat and tidy vampires I'd come to know.

Bet it was Rayne. He was no doubt planning my demise or, in the very least, a way to make my life there a living nightmare.

I snickered, remembering how Wynn had tossed him across the room so easily, then frowned at my hand. Damn. I wish I could do that. Maybe I could find me a pair of brass knuckles or maybe a boxing glove. There was little doubt in my mind that there wouldn't be a next time. Rayne was young and arrogant even if he was several decades older than me.

Sitting my pile of books on the nearby end table, I went through the stack. Greek mythology. My eyes scanned the shelves looking for the label for the myths.

There it was.

Shoving a few books onto the shelf, I moved to grab some more when my eyes caught the word vampire on the spine of one of the books. Reaching up onto my tiptoes to grab the book, I strained to get a hold of it. After a moment, I sighed and gave up, sinking back to my heels and turned to look for a stool.

"Shit!" I cried out, my hand going to my chest. A large figure stood inches from my shoulder. Once I got my heart to calm down, I glared at the large man with his intense gaze and buzzed haircut. Marcus. "Jeez, wear a bell or something. You nearly gave me a heart attack."

Marcus stared at me with increasing interest, his large muscular arms crossed over his chest pulling his dark green t-shirt tight over his pecs.

I waited for him to say something, tapping my foot impatiently, but when he obviously showed no intention of speaking, I threw my hands up and huffed, "Well? Did you need something?"

He stepped forward, and I froze, suddenly terrified I had offended him in some way. My feet backed up until my back hit the bookshelf behind me, making it slightly wobble. Breaths coming in and out like a frightened mouse, I squeezed my eyes shut and prepared myself for the worst.

A dark shadow fell over me, and for a moment, my senses were filled with lilacs and rain before it was gone. A few more moments passed, and I was still not dead or at least vampire chow, so I dared to open my eyes.

The first thing I noticed was the book, the exact one I had been reaching for, held out in front of me. The second thing was the amused hint of a smile on the edges of Marcus's mouth as his surveyed me.

Glancing between the book and then him again, my lips pursed tight. I hesitated before taking the book from him, clutching it to my chest. Bopping my head, I breathed in astonishment, "Thank you."

I thought he would leave after that, but he stood there for a moment before, in a low, gravelly voice, he asked, "You're staying?"

I arched a brow at him. "Uh, yes?" I didn't know why I made it a question. Like his opinion on it would change anything. My staying was between Antoine and myself. Okay and maybe Wynn, but he didn't need to know that.

Marcus nodded, a small jerky movement. "Good."

He didn't say anything else. Marcus turned on the heel of his combat boots and walked away. I couldn't help but let my eyes drift down to his backside where his jeans hugged his ass. I had to give it up for these vamps, they all have fabulous gluts.

Shaking my head, I laughed at my own lack of self-control. I glanced down at the book in my hands and moved over to the nearby couch. Checking to be sure no one else was going to sneak up on me, I cracked the book open. Of course, it was in Latin. A language I only recognized because of all the -uses.

I clapped the book shut and leaned back on the couch with a sigh. Just when I thought I might get some answer, I find the one vampire book that's in a dead language. Well, not like I had a lot of experience with vampire books. Not unless they involved shirtless alphas and whimpering damsels.

Wait a moment.

I was in a freaking paranormal romance.

Six sexy vampires with way more testosterone than any master vampire, and I'd already had more than one breathtaking encounter with them. All I needed was a display of jealousy that ended with us naked and sweaty.

Pfft. I should be so lucky.

Pushing off the couch, I went back to the shelf. Not bothering to try and reach that high up onto the bookshelf, I sat the book down and grabbed the nearby step stool. Of course, the one shelf that had something I wanted to read on it wasn't connected to the rolling ladder.

Sighing, I climbed onto the stool and put the book back where Marcus had gotten it.

"You know I could read it to you if you only asked," Drake announced, startling me. My foot missed the step on the stool, and my arms went out to my sides trying to grab onto something. Large arms wrapped around my waist and I found myself staring up at Allister. I only knew it was him because Drake stood behind him with a shit-eating grin on his face, his dimples flashing at me.

"Careful," Allister rumbled against me, the vibrations of it going straight through me. My nipples hardened, and I was in dire need of a new pair of panties. Jeez, it was ridiculous what these vamps could do with a few words and a bit of supernatural charm. Or maybe that was just their natural charm, and I was a simpering fool in desperate need of a good lay.

"Thanks," I murmured and withdrew myself from his arms and penetrating gaze, a bit reluctantly, I might add. Smoothing my hands down my shirt and pants, mostly to wipe my sweaty hands off, I peered between the two of them.

They really were almost identical. They both had dark hair that curled along the edges of their ears and those eyes, a swirling combination of blue and green with just a hint of golden flecks. Any girl would get lost in them. I had gotten lost in them. Well, Drake's but that was more of getting lost in his naked body and vampire tricks than his eyes. Now, that he was clothed... okay, who was I kidding? I still wanted to lick every inch of them, not that I'd tell that asshole as much. Drake, I mean, not Allister. The latter twin had yet to do anything to earn my ire.

"So, you want to know more about us, huh?" Drake snatched the book off the shelf where I just put it back. He flipped through a few pages and then pointed at a page, turning it around to face me. "This is a list of things that can kill us."

I squinted at the page, but it was all gibberish to me. Fat lot of good that list did when I couldn't read it. To the watching twins, I hummed. "Interesting."

Allister's lips quirked up, but he didn't comment. Drake smirked and flipped a few more pages. "And this page tells you how to become one of us if you were so inclined."

I cocked my head to the side and then up to his watchful eyes. "I'm not. However, I would like to know what I'm up against. Besides, your..." I waved my hand around in front of my face. "... you know, mind trick stuff, what else can you do? Are you really fast?" A memory came to my mind, and I held up my hand. "Wait, never mind. I know that one."

The twins exchanged a look but didn't pry further.

"Are you sure you have a reflection?" I tapped my chin. "I don't think I've ever seen any of you look in the mirror."

Allister sighed. "We're immortal, not invisible."

"What he said." Drake wrinkled his nose. "Some of the rumors really are a bit ridiculous, like the garlic bit. One person has an allergic reaction, and suddenly, it means all of us are." He dragged a hand through his hair, tousling it a bit before giving me a boyish grin. "Not that I would ever eat garlic. It puts a damper on the mood."

I didn't bother to ask what he meant by that, knowing I was just asking for trouble. Instead, I turned my next question to Allister. "So, you eat? Other things besides blood anyway."

Lifting a shoulder, Allister rolled his head making his bones crack. "We can, if we want to."

I remembered the cookie Rayne had eaten. "So, if you can eat regular food, why drink blood at all?"

"Because it tastes good," Drake cooed, moving around his brother to lean against the bookshelf. He was much closer now, close enough I could smell the heady musk coming off him. It made my knees weak and brought flashbacks of the time I had almost let him take me in his room, right up against his bedroom door. His vortex of color eyes seemed to swirl on their own as they trailed up and down my body, making my skin hot and needy. "I bet you taste oh so good."

Swallowing thickly, I jerked my eyes away from Drake to his twin, who watched with a curious frown. Did Allister not find me attractive? "What about you?"

Allister's eyes widened slightly as if not expecting me to pay any attention to him while his brother was making a move. "What about me?"

"Do you think I would taste good?" I cocked my head to the side, really wanting to know what he was thinking, especially since my question made Drake frown and back off a bit. "Or am I not your preferred flavor?"

Apparently, vampires could get embarrassed because Allister's face flushed a bright red, and his eyes ducked down to the hardwood floors. Scratching the back of his ear, he mumbled, "I'm not gay, if that's what you mean."

Drake threw his head back and laughed at his brother's discomfort. "Fuck, Al. Look at you. All bent out of shape because of one little maid." Drake's eyes darted over to me. "One really hot maid, but still, I haven't seen him this embarrassed since Ray asked if our dicks were identical too." I opened my mouth to ask, but Drake beat me to it. "And no, they're not."

I flushed and clipped my lips closed, lacing my fingers in front of me, my shoulders almost to my ears. "I had to ask."

"They all do," Drake drawled and then held the book out to me. "If you want to know anything, just ask. We'll be happy to help... for a price." The way his eyes lingered on my breasts told me exactly how he expected to be paid.

Allister didn't encourage or dissuade him, so I wasn't quite sure what his opinion was on the whole trading sex for information bit. Not that I could really say I wasn't tempted. Each of them alone was every woman's wet dream, but at the same time? I didn't think I had enough batteries to take care of that fantasy.

"I'll keep that in mind." I ducked my head, clutching the book to my chest as if it would hide how aroused I was at the prospect. I should just give up already. They knew everything about how I was feeling and, from Rayne's own mouth, my pitiful lifestyle. If I were a bolder woman, I would just embrace it but punching a vampire was as brave as I got, and look where that landed me!

CHAPTER 22

Drake

"DID YOU SMELL WHAT I smelled on her?" I asked my brother as the little maid ran away as fast as her little legs could carry her.

Allister shifted next to me, his nose sniffing the air. "There's something different about her, yes."

I scratched my chin. "She ran out of here pretty fast. Think we should be worried?"

My brother laughed. "You think too much."

Shoving his shoulder, I picked up the book Piper had been looking at. "And you don't worry enough."

Though we joked, there was something different about her, something that wasn't there before. I couldn't think of what could have made her scent change. It was subtle, barely noticeable if you weren't taking in lungfuls of her scent like I had been doing.

What could I say?

I was a creeper. I liked the taste of her on my lips and since I couldn't actually kiss her, not without freaking her out again, I would take what I could get.

"So, do you think Wynn will actually get her first?" Allister asked, flipping through a cook book. We rarely ate since our diet didn't require it, but for some reason, he was obsessed with food. If he had half a brain in his head, he'd use that to seduce the pretty maid.

Shrugging a shoulder, I shoved the book back on the shelf. "I don't know. Probably. He obviously has an advantage."

"I wonder if we should even be doing this." Allister sighed, he tucked the book he had and a few more under his arm. "Antoine already warned us to leave her alone, and then you go and fuck up. Isn't this pushing our luck?"

I snorted, heading for the library door. "When are we not pushing our luck?"

"Ha. Let's see you say that when you're begging to come home." Allister walked beside me, our footsteps echoing loudly as we make our way down the stairs. "I haven't heard him use that threat for a least a decade."

I waved him off. "Antoine just wants to fuck her, or he wouldn't be such a baby about us scaring her away."

"Oh, do I?"

Freezing in my steps, I winced. Me and my big mouth.

Slowly turning to the vampire in question, I offered a lazy grin. "Antoine, there you are. We were just talking about you."

"I heard." Antoine slid a hand through his long white hair, his pale eyes narrowing on me. I didn't let him know how fucking scared I was to go to our sire's. No one in their right mind would want to be with that lunatic. It was bad enough the first five years of my undead life. The further we got away from him, the better our lives had been.

"We were just discussing ways to make Miss Billings more comfortable here." Allister, ever the kiss ass, showed Antoine his books. "I thought maybe we could make her something to eat? Humans like food almost as much as sex," Allister ducked his eyes, and muttered, "or so I remember."

I smacked him on the back and laughed. "Look at him, all flustered about a girl."

"While I appreciate the sentiment," Antoine pursed his lips, giving me a warning look, "I think more distance from Miss

Billings might be a better solution. However, we have another matter to discuss." He turned on his heel and walked into the dining room without waiting to see if we followed.

Arrogant bastard.

"What happened here?" I frowned at the mirror shattered on the ground.

Darren had a broom in his hand sweeping up the pieces. He glanced up from the ground to meet my gaze, a grim expression on his face. "Another gift from your favorite little maid. First the Qing, now the Lalique. I think she might be doing it on purpose now."

"Why would she do that?" Allister asked, putting a bit of power into his voice, making Darren's shoulders scrunch up like a turtle trying to pull his head back into his shell.

No one liked to fuck with Darren as much as Allister did. He was a nice guy for the most part, but besides Antoine, Darren treated the rest of us like naughty children who needed to listen to their parents. I didn't know if he meant him or Antoine, but either way, it only put a target on his back for our mischief.

Antoine snapped his finger, knocking Darren out of Allister's trance before shooting us a glare. Sliding into his chair at the head of the dining room table, he sighed. "Perhaps she has found a reason to stay and the only way she can think to make sure she won't be fired is to owe us more?"

I snorted.

"You find this funny?" Antoine angled his head toward me.

Flopping down in my chair a few seats away from him, I shrugged. "I just think you give Piper too much credit."

"Miss Billings," he corrected me.

Waving him off, I leaned forward and cupped my hands in front of me. "It's less likely that she actually thinks that and more likely that she's a klutz. She almost killed herself in the library a few minutes ago getting a book."

Antoine's brow shot up to his hair line and then turned his gaze to Allister. "Is this true?"

Allister sat next to me, his shoulders stiff. He didn't put the books on the table but sat them on the floor next to him. "I caught her."

"Hmm." Antoine watched us for a moment before moving his gaze to Darren. "Which do you think it is? An unfortunate mishap or a calculated move?"

Darren let out a rude sound. "If you spent more than five minutes in a room with Miss Billings, you'll know she doesn't have a calculating bone in her body. No, if anything, she broke it simply to spite me than to stay here longer. I actually have the feeling she'd rather get a different job but is unable to for some reason."

The butler's assessment made me frown. That couldn't be right. She was a gorgeous woman with plenty of going for her. There's no way she has to be a maid. I guess if she didn't have any other skills to fall back on, that would be a problem, but if I were her, I'd have found me a rich husband and never work a day in my life.

Women these days.

"Any other comments?" Antoine asked Darren and then glanced back my way.

I grinned and shifted in my seat. "Yeah, she's giving me a perpetual case of blue balls. Can we do something about that?"

Antoine's lip curled up in disgust. "Yes, be an adult and go take care of it yourself."

"What? You're not offering up your servant for the job?" I let my eyes linger on Darren who had an unreadable expression on his face.

It wasn't a secret the two of them dallied with each other from time to time. I didn't know if they actually cared for one another or it if was simply because their blood bond required it. Either way, it gave me great pleasure to poke at the otherwise serious pair.

"I'm going to pretend you didn't say that," Antoine calmly stated, tapping his finger on the top of the table. "Now, Darren, what's for dinner?"

The butler's shoulders sagged. The movement was so slight if you hadn't been looking for it, you wouldn't have noticed. I was watching and I did notice. I repressed a grin.

Another point for me.

CHAPTER 23

Piper

"OH, MY GOD." I closed my eyes and moaned around the mouthful of chicken overtaking my mouth. "Dear Lord, Gretchen you've outdone yourself this time."

The older woman chuckled, wiping her hands on a dish towel. "Why thank you, Piper, but honestly, it's the same old chicken I always make. The masters don't really seem to want much variety in my dishes." She and Darren, who sat next to me at the countertop, exchanged a look.

I shook my head and cut a larger piece of the succulent meat. "I'm telling you, I've had your chicken before, and this is so much better." I popped the piece I'd cut into my mouth, rolling it around as I chewed. The juice and seasoning filled every inch of my mouth. "It's like an explosion of flavor."

The two of them watched me with growing interest, but I ignored them and continued eating. Who cared if they stared? I liked food. Good food. And I've never tasted anything so good as the chicken before me. Maybe because it was the first real thing I'd eaten since waking up from my nap. Strangely enough, I hadn't been hungry after drinking Wynn's blood, a concept that still weirded me out.

"You seem in better spirits today, all things considering." The caution in Darren's voice made me pause. Was he afraid I'd run screaming into the night?

I lifted a shoulder and dropped it, tucking into the roasted potatoes next. "I don't know what you expect really. As long as they keep their fangs to themselves and aren't killing anyone, it's not really any different than the rest of the weirdos out there."

Gretchen laughed, a full belly laugh. Rubbing her eyes with the back if her hand, she bobbed her head. "I'm glad you feel that way. We've lost plenty of good maids because of the masters' peculiarities," she drew out with a wink.

Darren snorted. "More like had to get rid of them. Either they were too terrified to stay, or they wanted to be one of them. I blame the media. Too many glittery vampires and angsty teenager books and movies. Takes the real fear out of what they should be wary of." He gave me a pointed look.

I swallowed the potato in my mouth and picked up my glass of water. "Believe me, I'm wary, far more than you know." My eyes brows rose, and my eyes rolled, remembering my few encounters with the masters. I'd have to be stupid not to keep in mind what they were or take the chance of turning into someone's chew toy.

"It's not just their teeth you have to be aware of," Darren started but then clipped his mouth shut. He spun around in his chair and greeted Rayne as he walked into the kitchen. "Can I get you anything?"

How he knew Rayne was coming before he even appeared, I chalked up to having something to do with that blood bond keeping him young and healthy. However, the total disregard Rayne had for Darren pissed me off. The redhead moved into the kitchen, his eyes flickering to me for a millisecond, the heat in them scorching me to the bone. He stopped in front of the fridge and jerked the door open. Rayne stared in there for way longer than needed before grabbing his usual silver container.

The rest of us were quiet all the while, watching him and waiting to see if he would deem us worthy of his notice.

Gretchen smiled at him as he turned around and offered him a plate. "Would you like some chicken to go with your drink?"

Twisting the cap off, Rayne ignored her and met my gaze, leaning against the counter as he chugged the liquid.

Not wanting him to know he affected me, I returned his glare with a quirk of my lips and an arched brow. To my delight, his eyes narrowed, and he lowered the container, dark red dripping from the side of his mouth.

"You have some..." I pointed at the side of my mouth. "Right there." Having a death wish, I picked up my napkin and threw it at him. His hand shot up and caught it in a tight grip, probably imagining my head was the napkin.

Wiping his mouth quickly, he slammed the container on the counter which made Gretchen jump, her brows furrowing and a deep frown on her lips. Darren stiffened beside me as Rayne stomped over to the island.

"Your hand." He stared down at the hand I had thrown the napkin with, the one with the wrap around it even though I didn't need it.

The one he had broken.

"What about it?" I stabbed a potato and popped it into my mouth, the edges of my eyes crinkling.

Those amber eyes zeroed in on it, and before I could register it, he had moved. Rayne had my hand in his grasp and jerked me half way across the table, my plate getting shoved to the side.

"Hey, let go!"

Rayne ignored me and turned my hand this way and that as if it were some kind of medical wonder. "Why isn't it still broken?"

Gretchen made a small sound in between a gasp and a cry, her eyes darting to me. I shook my head as if to tell her I'd talk to her about it later. I didn't want her to get in trouble with the dick head, not because of me.

"Wynn took care of it, no thanks to you." I jerked my hand out of his partially, surprised he let me, and sat back in my seat. My lips twisted into a grimace at the mess my shirt had turned into.

Rayne stared at me for a moment, not understanding what I meant until his brows shot to his hairline and he snarled. "He gave you his blood."

It wasn't a question, so I didn't answer it, focusing on cleaning myself off the best I could.

When he appeared at my elbow, I didn't have the chance to argue. His hand clamped down on my arm and pulled me once again out of my seat, except this time, he practically dragged me across the kitchen and into the dining room where the other brothers sat at the table.

The room went deathly quiet. Rayne threw me forward, and if I hadn't been expecting him to be an ass, I'd have severely injured myself on the table's edge.

"Tell him what you did." I thought Rayne was talking to me, but his eyes were on Wynn, not me.

I glanced up from where I laid halfway across the table, my hands curled over the edges of the wood. Antoine's pale eyes watched me with a bland expression, not giving away what he was thinking while the twins had matching amused grins. Marcus... well, who knew what Marcus was thinking half the time?

"I don't know what you are talking about." Wynn swirled the dark liquid in his wine glass. This time it seemed to be actual wine and not blood. Guess the twins were telling the truth, they did eat other things.

Rayne growled behind me, but this time, I was ready for him. I ducked out of his grasp and moved away from him, shifting closer to where Wynn sat. "Don't touch me."

Antoine's cultured voice rang out through the dining room, jerking Rayne's attention from me to his older brother. "What is the meaning of this?"

Snapping his teeth, Rayne threw a hand in my direction before crossing his arms over his chest. "Wynn gave her some of his blood."

I felt more than saw the masters' eyes move to me. Wynn was the only one not looking at me, still staring at his glass a nonchalant kind of way.

"Wynn?" Antoine clipped, those eyes finally moving off me and onto his brother. "Is this true?"

Wynn sighed. "Yes. I did. Now if we're tattling," Drake snickered at his brother's words, "why don't you tell them why I had to give Piper my blood, little brother?"

Rayne froze.

I chewed on my lower lip, fidgeting in place. I wasn't sure why Wynn giving me his blood was a big deal, but I knew the fact that Rayne had hurt me wasn't a good thing. Or at least I hoped so. Wynn had seemed to be on my side, but I didn't know the rest of them well enough to confidently say one way or the other if they cared if I were hurt.

"Rayne. I'm waiting."

The redhead scoffed and turned his head away from Antoine's piercing gaze.

"Perhaps Miss Billings would be so kind as to illuminate to us what our dear brother has done? Did he hurt you?"

"Uh... not exactly." I twisted my hands in front of me. I didn't really want to get into it. If I told them about how I broke my hand, then they'll want to know why and then Rayne would tell them about my dream.

Rayne still didn't answer his brother. Probably didn't want to get hit again. Not that I blamed him.

"Rayne, do not make me ask again. What happened?" Antoine laced his fingers in front of him on the table, his eyes locked onto us.

The redhead vampire clenched his jaw and bit out. "She broke her hand."

"And how did she do that?" Wynn prompted, a hint of a smile on his lips.

Scowling at him, Rayne jerked his head to the side and muttered, "Punching my face."

Drake and Allister busted out laughing, banging on the table hard enough to make me jump in place. Marcus even lowered his guard enough to show amusement in his eyes.

Antoine cocked a brow at me, a smile teasing his lips. "Miss Billings, what was Rayne doing to cause this need for violence?"

"Me?" Rayne snapped. "What makes you think I did anything?"

Antoine's eyes zeroed in onto Rayne. "One hundred and fifty years of experience." His gaze softened as he moved his gaze back to me, gesturing with a hand for me to continue. "Miss Billings?"

I licked my lips, my eyes darting to Rayne who glowered at me and then to Wynn who gave me a small, encouraging incline of his head. "I was taking a nap and forgot to lock my door." I paused at the hum that released from Antoine's throat. I could feel my face heating up as I fumbled through the rest of my explanation. "Uh..." I cleared my throat and shifted from side to side. "I... uh..."

"Just spit it out already," Rayne griped. "I came onto her, and she punched me. That's it, okay?" He moved his eyes to Antoine and Wynn, then the rest of his brothers before nodding his head with a firm jerk. "Fine. It's over. Now you can't tell me that's worse than giving a complete stranger some of our blood?"

The question was for Antoine, and it wasn't taken lightly.

It was really a peculiar thing, how still he became. If I hadn't been looking at him, I wouldn't have even known he was there. His face looked like the granite Rayne's had felt like when I broke my hand. I did not envy whoever that look was for.

"While I don't approve of Rayne's actions, as deplorable as they are," those liquid steel eyes zipped to Rayne who had the decency to duck his head in shame, "Miss Billings has only been part of this household for less than two weeks. Wynn, what made you think it would be acceptable to share something so important with someone who doesn't know our ways?"

Wynn lifted an elegant shoulder and then his lips curled up in a lopsided grin. "Perhaps I saw something in Piper worth the risk."

"You think this is funny?" Rayne slammed his hands on the table. "Do you want another human leashed to us for eternity?"

For a moment, I wondered who Rayne was talking about, but the only one I could think of was Darren. Would I be like him now? My eyes widened, and I whipped around to gap at Wynn.

"That's not one of those side effects you were warning me about?"

However, it wasn't Wynn who answered but Drake. "Well, that depends."

"On what?"

"How much of his blood did you drink?"

I lifted my fingers up making my thumb and forefinger the size of the vial about two inches.

"Barely a swallow." Wynn waved his hand languidly.

Drake blew a long breath out, rolling his eyes. "Hardly worth the argument."

I let out a sigh. Obviously, I wasn't in any threat of becoming immortal from the tiny amount I had, but still, I worried about the side effects. "What kind of things could happen?"

Allister tapped his fingers on the table. "Increased senses, including sensitivity to light."

"Food tastes better," Drake added.

Ah. That made sense. No wonder Darren and Gretchen looked at me like I was a psycho.

Antoine made a sound in his throat and for a second seemed uncomfortable with the conversation. "You may find yourself attracted to Wynn as well as having a generally heightened libido."

I almost laughed out loud, like I could be any more into him than I already felt. If my naughty dreams lately were any indication of being a sex deprived deviant, I couldn't imagine it getting any worse.

Getting out of my own thoughts, I noticed the room had grown quiet. Tense. All eyes were on me.

My pulse flared, and I suddenly felt naked in the middle of a room full of hungry vampires. Taking a deep breath, I forced myself to calm down. Chill out. They don't know what you're thinking if you don't let your body give it away.

Licking my lips, I laced my fingers behind my back and started to back out of the room. "If you don't need anything else, I'm just going to…"

"Miss Billings."

Fuck.

"Yes, Master Durand?" I avoided his gaze at all costs staring hard at the hardwood floor.

"We're having another get together this next weekend."

Fuck, another one? "I'll be sure to be more prepared this time." Meaning I'd stay in my room with doors locked and crosses at the ready.

"Actually, we would like you to help Darren serve the room if you think you're up for it." My head jerked up and my eyes locked with Antoine's.

After a second, I picked my jaw up off the floor and nodded my head rapidly. "Yes, of course. I'd be happy to."

Picking up his wine glass, he released my gaze to take a sip. I assumed that meant I was dismissed and took the chance to dash out of there.

Darren and Gretchen waited in the kitchen, not bothering to be stealthy about their eavesdropping.

Clasping my hands on my cheeks, I shook my head from side to side. "What the hell just happened?"

CHAPTER 24

Antoine

A BURNING RAGE FILLED me. It flowed through my blood as I clenched my jaw tight. I was the master of my own actions. I would not succumb to the violence within me.

"Do you think what you did was wise?" I bit out as Rayne sat down in his chair at the end of the table. "We are trying to gain her trust, not destroy it in a single instance."

I couldn't help the sharpness to my tone as my anger started to get out of control. Sucking in a breath, I steeled myself, finding the center of perfect balance. He was just a child playing at being a full-grown man, let alone a mature vampire.

Sometimes I wondered what our sire was thinking when he made this lot.

Actually, I knew what he had been thinking. Nothing. Like he did with all his creations. He simply found someone interesting or attractive and changed them, with or without their permission.

I'd learned that the hard way when he took me under his wing. Then I spent every day of my undead life fighting to get out from under it and run things my own way. Now that I finally had my own house, I wasn't about to ruin it by letting my brothers in blood get out of control.

"She pisses me off." Rayne pouted, crossing his arms over his chest.

I wanted to give him the benefit of the doubt. After all, I couldn't read minds. How was I to know what he'd been seeing inside that woman's head? However, a point had to be made.

"If we all got to do whatever we wanted just because someone irked us, I'd have staked you lot a long time ago."

Draconius and Allister snickered, earning them a glowering stare. They hushed up but didn't stop smiling. The idiot twins. I didn't know what possessed me to allow them to come with me to build my house.

Oh, I remember. I was a sucker.

They were abused far more than the rest of us underneath our sire's delicate hand. No one knew how to push boundaries like our sire did. It was no wonder they had rushed to accept my offer of joining my house as easily as they had.

My hand reached up and palmed my chest, right above my heart where my own house tattoo sat. When we were all full of optimism and joy for our new house and freedom, we'd gotten matching ink. Some days, it was a reminder of what we had broken away from. Other days, like today, it reminded me to have patience and compassion. They needed me as I needed them. Blood of my blood, now and forever.

"Oh, come now, Antoine. You know you'd be lonely without us here." Wynn smirked, lounging in his chair like he had no cares in the world.

Sadly, I knew differently. The flirty vampire might act like nothing bothered him, but I knew what the sire had him use his powers for.

"I have Darren," I reminded him, not playing his game. "He is far better company and gives less lip."

Wynn opened his mouth to retort, and I held up a hand. "Forget it. I set myself up for that. Keep your comments to yourself. Anyone else want to bring up new business while we are at the table?" I laced my finger and glanced around the room.

Surprisingly the one who answered was Marcus. The quiet stoic mountain of a man who acted as my unofficial guard during formal events shifted beside me. "Yes, Marcus?"

"Is it wise to allow an unclaimed human to attend?"

I didn't need to ask Marcus what he meant. He was a man of few words, but when he did speak, he only spoke what was necessary to portray his point, a very good one in this instance.

"I'm with Marcus." Rayne sniffed and then scowled, probably listening into someone's thoughts. "The maid isn't marked. She's untrained in our ways and will only be a liability."

"Then perhaps you should be the one to instruct her?" I countered, almost smiling at the way the redhead froze in his chair. "You seem so concerned with her wellbeing, after all, so maybe you should be in charge of making sure she is presentable and acts accordingly."

This time Wynn spoke up, his usual carefree expression pensive. "But Valentine and Theresa are coming."

He didn't need to explain further. We all knew what those two coming would mean. Our sire was sending his lap dogs to check up on us, make sure there were no reason to dissolve our household... or maybe make a reason. One never knew with him.

"Yes. Valentine is coming." I crossed a leg over the other and leaned forward to catch their eyes. "Which means we play their game. No need to bring attention to ourselves or give them an excuse to drag us back to the main household."

"Then why let Piper come at all?" Drake asked.

This time I let a slow smile slide up my face. "Because Valentine would be suspicious if we didn't have a maid, even more so if we hid her away." I paused for effect. "He might think we have other things to hide, and we cannot have that."

The others grumbled their agreement and I thought that would be the end of it.

"Mark her."

My head swiveled Marcus, surprised he would make the suggestion. "Why? She has not proven herself trustworthy."

Wynn snorted. "She knows we're vampires and yet stays. Is that not trustworthy enough?"

Rayne made a rude sound in his throat. "You only want her marked because you are already one step into being blood bonded. What's a bit of fang action going to hurt?"

Wynn glared at Rayne. "Says the one who got punched because they were jealous and pushed her too far."

Jumping out of his seat, Rayne banged his fists on the table. "I am not jealous."

Sliding his eyes to the side, Wynn gave a small shrug. "Says the one not in her dreams."

I placed my face in my hand, shaking it slightly. And around and round we go.

"Enough." I pushed a bit of power into my voice, causing Rayne and Wynn to stop bickering. Rayne slumped down in his seat, and Wynn merely went back to smirking.

Standing from my own chair, I placed a finger on the table. "If you have an issue with Miss Billings, you will remedy it before this weekend. I don't need you lot airing our dirty laundry in front of Valentine."

Rayne opened his mouth to argue, but I pushed even more power out until the room filled with it. A human would have choked on the amount, falling to their knees before me.

"You will find her suitable attire and teach her what she should and shouldn't do. I am leaving Miss Billings' welfare in your hands." Rayne gaped at me as I continued. "If Valentine lays a single hand on her, it will be you who pays."

The unspoken question was met by a chorus of nods.

Satisfied with their agreement, I adjusted my cuffs and moved away from the table. "Now, I need to release some of this energy before I bring the house down. Who will join me for a hunt?"

It was not surprising that the whole table stood with me. We were all a bit on edge, and the reason being was only a paltry hundred and twenty pounds of blonde simpering flesh.

Oh, how the mighty have fallen.

CHAPTER 25

Piper

THE LIGHTS OF THE shops broke through the darkness and made me sigh. I'd spent too much time in the Durand Manor and not enough time out with the living. It was the day before the party I was supposed to help with, and I had finally gotten done early.

Maybe I was getting better at the job?

Images of Rayne's pink underwear coming out of the wash made my lips quirk up. Nope, guess I wasn't. Still, even though it had been an accident, imagining the rage on the redhead's face when he found out was more than worth it. Little prick.

I needed this night out of the house, especially if I was going to be surrounded by not just all six of the vampire masters but strangers as well.

After my weird encounter with the masters, one would think the rest of the week would go on like normal, and for the most part, it did. I woke up at seven, found the note under my door from Darren for the daily chores, then went about doing said chores.

The only difference was the dreams.

If I thought my dreams were naughty before, they had turned XXX-rated in ways I could have never in my wildest dreams have thought of. Each and every one of those dreams featured Wynn. Sure, the others had cameos here and there, but Wynn was the one whispering sweet nothings in my ears before he plunged inside of me with cock and fangs. I'd wake up a shaking mess and in desperate need of new panties.

I'd already gone through a whole box of batteries from how bad it has gotten. However, I made sure to keep my door locked and to only do it during the daytime hours. No need to draw even more attention to my room than I already have.

Avoiding Wynn had been a different challenge altogether. It seemed that I wasn't the only one who had grown attracted, or in my case even more attracted, to the other.

Where before Wynn wouldn't be up and around before the sun had set, I now would find him reading in his room when I came around to get the laundry.

I darted into the drug store as this morning's incident flared up in my mind.

"What are you reading?" I couldn't help but ask. I stood in the doorway of his room, his laundry bag sagging in my hand.

Wynn lounged on his bed, one leg propped up and an arm behind his head, his tantalizing eyes focused solely on the book in his hand. Without looking up from his book, Wynn answered, "The Odyssey."

"Oh."

Oh? Piper. Really? Way to make yourself look like an illiterate idiot.

I shifted from side to side before giving up on trying to find something impressive to say and headed for his laundry basket. I cursed and chastised myself under my breath, shoving handfuls of clothes into the bag. The scent of Wynn wafted up from the clothes, and my insides tightened involuntarily. I stifled a moan, rubbing my legs together to ease the ache.

My face flushed, realizing I was getting turned on just by his dirty laundry. What the fuck?

"Piper." Wynn's usual flirty tone had turned dark and sultry in my ear.

Freezing in place, my back tensed hard enough to break bone. Had he caught me? Did he know how much I wanted him?

Swallowing and then licking my lips, I slowly turned to face him. "Uh, yes?"

With a bemused sort of grin, Wynn stood in the bathroom doorway, his head angled to the side. "Did you just sniff my clothes?"

Yep. He'd seen me.

Tucking a stray blonde hair behind my ear, I ducked my head and glanced down at the bag in my hand. "Uh. Not on purpose. Kind of hard not to notice."

"And?"

My head jerked up. "And what?"

"Do I smell bad?"

Narrowing my eyes at the laughter in his voice, I wrinkled my nose. "Like an old dirty gym sock. You really should get that checked out or buy some deodorizer for your shoes."

Wynn's blue eyes had turned dark and stormy, and his fangs peeked out from his lips, something that he usually hid so well until now. "Is that so?" He prowled toward me, much like the first day we had met, like a panther closing in on his prey.

Frozen in place, my hand closed and opened on the bag of laundry, not sure how to react to this beast I'd unleashed.

Did I run? No, he'd just chase me.

Play dead? I had a feeling that wouldn't work. Heightened senses made for better hearing, and I wasn't one of those people who could slow their heart rate at will.

Hands slammed into the walls on either side of me hard enough to scare me. "Your mind is elsewhere, little human. I thought we were bonding here."

My eyes skittered away from his arms caging me into his tantalizing gaze. My tongue snuck out to wet my lips, and Wynn's eyes followed the movement. I let out a nervous laugh and fiddled with the edge of my t-shirt. "Uh...were we?"

His lips curled up in a wolfish manner as he leaned into me. "Yes, you were about to tell me how badly I smell."

"Was I?" I murmured, only barely paying mind to what he was saying. I'd never been this close to him before. Our breaths mingled, and I could say with all surety that he did not stink, breath or otherwise. He was close enough to kiss if I just moved an inch. My eyelids fluttered, and I prepared myself to be kissed.

"So?"

"So, what?" My eyes snapped back open, confusion filling me. Wynn had his head tilted to the side, so his neck was bare to me. Did he want me to bite him?

He let out an impatient sigh. "What do I smell like?"

Oh. Freaking literal much.

I released the laundry bag and placed my hand on his shoulder and pushed up on my toes, giving his neck a quick whiff before backing away.

"Well?"

A mixture of jasmine and thunderstorms assaulted my senses, sinking deep inside of me. My breasts felt heavy and ached for his touch. But I didn't tell him that. Or that my panties were practically ruined from just the smell of him.

With as much self-restraint as I could muster which, let's face it, wasn't much, I stepped back from him, picked my bag up, and muttered, "You smell fine," before ducking under his arm and running from the room.

I'd been avoiding him ever since.

"Do you need help finding something?" a small shop girl with freckles and a pretty smile asked me, jerking me out of my thoughts. Her name tag told me that her name was June.

I returned her smile and let out a nervous laugh. I'd been staring at the same bottle of shampoo for who knew how long so she probably thought I was going to steal the damn thing. "No, sorry. I just forgot what I came for."

June's eyes crinkled around the edges. "Boy troubles?"

Sighing, I put the shampoo back on the shelf. "How'd you know?"

"You have that look."

I cocked my head to the side. "What look?"

Waving a hand at my face, she explained, "Dazed. Jumpy. Lack of normal motor functions."

Giggling, I scratched my ear. "Is it that obvious?"

June leaned into me. "No, but I know the signs. So why don't you tell me about it? I might be able to help, and if not, I can at least offer my expertise in hair care." She winked, making me laugh again.

I ran my hand up and down my purse strap, staring at the shampoos. "Well, I like this guy."

"Okay, a male." June nodded with all seriousness. "We're getting somewhere. So, does he know you exist?"

Despite myself, I grinned. "Oh, yeah."

"And he likes you?"

"I think so."

June pursed her lips and placed her hands on her hips. "So, what's the deal?"

"Well..." I drew out, trying to figure out how to explain it. I couldn't very well just spit out that he's a vampire, one of six hotter than should be legal ones that I worked for, and while I would love nothing more than to ride him like a bull, I wasn't sure I wanted to get that involved with him or any of them for that matter. Immortal soul pending aside, Wynn didn't seem the long-term commitment kind. If he were, then he'd want me to be like him too, and I was so not ready for that. "He's kind of my boss."

"Ooo." June rubbed her hands together with glee. "A forbidden work romance. I like it."

I ducked my head, scuffing my shoe on the laminate floor. "Yeah."

"So, he's your boss."

"Well, kind of. He's the brother of the head of the... company, and I'd already been warned not to get involved with them... because it's against company policy." Okay, so I was stretching it, but that was close enough to right.

June bobbed her head up and down a thoughtful look on her face. "Understandable. So, you have to decide. Do you like him or just want him to defile you in the best of ways?"

I barked a laugh. "What?"

"Like," she let out an impatient breath, "do you actually like him, or do you just want to bone him? Can you have a one and done? Get him out of your system and get back to work?"

I thought about it for a moment. Could I do that? Could I screw Wynn and be completely over it? A delectable shudder ran through me at the thought of being with the dark-haired vampire.

Letting out a shaky breath, I shook my head. "No, no way."

"Then you have to quit."

"What?" My eyes widened. "I can't do that."

June shrugged. "Well, that's how I see it. Either quit so you can be together, or suck it up and... hold on." She ran back to her counter, grabbed something from the top of it, and came back over. Smacking it in my hand, she grinned. It was a pack of batteries. "Buy a whole lot of those."

I was just about to tell her that was exactly what I had planned before a voice I didn't expect to hear called out. "There you are."

Holding back a groan, I slowly turned to Rayne. He stood with Allister and Drake behind him, almost like they were his bodyguards for how big they were in comparison. Drake had an amused grin on his lips while Allister seemed way too interested in the drug store like he'd never been to one before. Rayne, the little prick, had a perpetual scowl on his lips as if I were wasting his time.

I glanced back at June. Her eyes were as wide as saucers, and her mouth gaped open. Offering her a polite smile, I nodded to the batteries. "Thank you for these and the advice."

Starting to walk away, June grabbed my arm and pulled me close. "Forget what I said. Risk it. It'll be worth it, I promise."

I frowned at her and then realized she thought Rayne was the guy I was into. I started to correct her but said guy jerked me by the arm and all I could do was wave. "Hold on, I have to pay for these."

"Forget it." Rayne threw some money on the counter as we passed by, and I offered an apologetic look before being dragged out of the store.

Once we were on the sidewalk, I yanked my arm away from him, rubbing it while I glared at him. "What the hell was that about? This is my time off."

Drake and Allister came up behind him, now more interested in our argument than anything. Rayne tucked his hands into the back pockets of his jeans. "Not anymore. Antoine wants us to find you something suitable to wear for tomorrow night. Let's go."

"And why can't I get something on my own? And what's with the backup? One of you isn't enough?" I snapped, shoving the batteries into my purse.

Placing a hand on his chest, Drake gaped. "I'm hurt, and here I thought we were being nice, keeping our little brother from killing you in a public place."

"So, you're babysitting."

"What?" Rayne clipped. "They are not babysitting me."

Allister snorted.

I rolled my eyes. "If he needs a sitter, then why send him at all? There are six of you. Clearly one of you could have come on your own. Or even Darren."

"Believe me, I'm not any happier about it than you." Rayne turned on his heels and started walking down the sidewalk.

Drake stared after his brother, before turning to me. "Darren did offer, but Antoine thinks you two need to clear the air."

"Besides," Allister added with a small smile, "Rayne has the best taste in women's clothing."

"He does, does he?" I drew out, letting my eyes trail after him.

I didn't know why but something inside of me twisted tight and not in a good way. Why did the thought of the jerk face picking out clothes for other women rub me so wrong? It wasn't like I liked him. I liked Wynn. Okay, maybe Antoine a bit too. The twins weren't bad either. Marcus was sweet in his quietly imposing way. But not Rayne! He'd done nothing but be an ass to me.

"Come on, before the little baby throws a hissy fit." Drake gave me a bit of a push toward the way Rayne had headed.

I snorted. At least I wasn't the only one who saw him as an oversized baby. Now, if I could keep myself from wringing his neck long enough to find something suitable to wear for tomorrow.

Good fucking luck.

CHAPTER 26

Piper

"I MEAN, THIS IS the— Actually, I don't. Hell, no," I snapped, jerking the curtain of the dressing room open. I hit my hands against the fluffy, layered black skirt and scowled. "I'm not wearing this."

Drake leered at me, not even hiding his pleasure. "I like it."

"Of course, you do. You're into this kind of crap." I tugged at the lace choker and grimaced, feeling feminism going back a hundred years just for agreeing to put the dress on.

"What kind of person is that?" Allister made a small sound in his throat, half between a laugh and a hum. If he knew what was good for him, he'd not draw my ire in his direction. I had plenty to go around starting with the sadist ass wipe who thought this was a good idea.

"Seriously?" I shot back, my brow raising to my forehead. "I look like a Gothic Lolita." I grimaced, pulling on the tight corset top half of the dress. If I were a bigger girl or buxomer, there would be no chance of getting me into this contraption. I was dying here.

"Stop bitching. Here, put these on." Rayne came around the corner of the dressing area, holding a pair of black heeled Mary Janes and white, thigh-high tights. He shoved them into my arm, but I pushed them back, earning me a frown. "What?"

"I'm not wearing this. I'm the maid, not some vampire pin-up girl."

Drake snorted.

"Watch it." I shot him a glare.

Rayne wasn't affected by my words. "You'll wear it because I was put in charge of dressing you. Darren has never complained about my clothing choices."

My fingers curled into fists, and I bared my teeth. "That's because his outfit didn't come with frilly underpants."

Letting out a disparaging sigh, Rayne raised his eyes to the ceiling. "No one said you had to wear the underwear." I opened my mouth to argue, and Rayne pressed a hand to my mouth. "Let me put it in a way you will understand. Others like us aren't as forward thinking. They won't see you as an equal."

"You're food to them," Drake interjected.

"Exactly." Rayne nodded to his brother. "They won't bother to ask if you want to be touched or groped. Wouldn't you rather have piles of fabric between you and their grabby hands?"

My brows scrunched together. He made sense... surprisingly. Damn it.

"Fuck, fine. Give them to me." Rayne handed over the stockings and shoes with a smug look that I wanted to smack off. Instead, I ducked behind the curtain and threw my skirt up to pull on the thigh highs. "If this is all to keep them from getting handsy, why wear a skirt at all? Or the choker?"

"The guests coming are old fashioned. Women wear dresses and men wear pants. You won't want to give them the impression that you aren't a lady, despite the obvious." Rayne's voice rolled over the curtain, and I could just imagine the snarky expression on his face. Man, I wanted to hit him again, broken hand be damned. It was worth it.

I held onto that feeling as I finished rolling up the tights. They were actually cute, if I were honest. The tops of them were frilly with black bows landing just above my knee. The shoes were thankfully only a couple of inches with thick heels. If I had to be on my feet all night, I'd rather be comfortable.

I pushed the curtain back open and held my hands out to my sides. "Well?"

Rayne's eyes scanned over me, a finger tapping his chin as he circled me like a damn vulture. My fingers curled around the fabric of the poufy skirt, not knowing what to do with them while he surveyed me.

"You'll do," Rayne finally announced, stopping in front of me.

"Good. Then I can take this crap off." I shifted to go back into the dressing room, but Rayne stopped me with his hand. His other hand reached up and touched the lace collar around my neck. The collar and the thin straps of the dress were the only things covering my shoulders and neck, the neckline of the dress barely dipping to hint at a cleavage. It was a weird combination of conservative and tempting.

"The collar is to give the illusion that you have been claimed."

I cocked my head to the side, glancing around him to the twins. "Claimed?"

Drake nodded. "While our family adheres to a different set of rules, others will expect us to have... tasted you."

I shivered at the way he said it, not completely displeased by the prospect.

"If you aren't bound to our family then you are a threat or food." Rayne adjusted the strap of my dress, and I smacked his hand away with a glower. Not at all bothered by my lashing out, Rayne ran a hand through his red hair, tousling it. "The collar hides the fact that you haven't been bitten though it might not stop some of them from trying for you."

Allister snorted. "Valentine."

"Exactly." Rayne's head jerked once.

Sighing at all the vampire bullshit, I threw my hands up. "Then why even have me serve? Darren is used to doing it all by himself, isn't he?"

"Yes," Rayne exchanged a look with his brothers, "but Antoine wants you there and what he says goes."

He didn't seem entirely happy about that, but I didn't probe. I took the chance to duck into the dressing room and ripped the outfit off as fast as I could without destroying it in the process. I'd already peeked at the price tag and about threw up when I saw the four digits. Who the hell spent that much on a single outfit, let alone one they didn't want?

Putting my regular jeans and t-shirt back on, I gathered up the outfit and handed it over to Rayne to pay for. He took it up to the front counter where an overly enthusiastic female clerk rushed to help him. Drake and Allister hung back with me as we waited for him to finish paying. The more Rayne tried to leave, the more the woman, who looked around his age if he wasn't a vampire permanently stuck as a twenty-year-old, flirted with him.

He just couldn't seem to get away without being a dick.

"Why doesn't he just tell her to fuck off?" I muttered, getting annoyed.

Drake chuckled. "Because Rayne isn't that kind of guy."

My mouth dropped open. "Not that kind of guy? He hated on me the moment I stepped into the house. If anyone could tell someone to fuck off, it'd be him."

Drake and Allister exchanged a look and just laughed, irritating me more.

After a moment, the clerk wrote something on a paper and handed it to Rayne. Reluctantly, Rayne took the paper and made a show of putting it in his pocket before taking the bag she was holding hostage and coming back to us.

"Ready?"

"Are you?" I crossed my arms and cocked my hip to the side. "Or did you need to suck face with the clerk first?"

Rayne gave me a quizzical look before shaking his head. "Whatever. I'm hungry. Let's find something to eat then go home." I tried to reach for the bag, but he wouldn't let me take it, insisting he carried it.

Stomping after him, my mind a jumbled mess of confusion, I waved an arm toward where my car sat. "Why can't we just eat at home? My car's down there."

"Because I'm tired of microwaved meals." Rayne ignored my directions and headed for an Italian place across the street.

The twins looped their arms through mine, effectively giving me no choice but to come with them.

"Come on, Piper." Drake crooned in my ear. "Spend time with us. It's not like you get to see us much around the house."

I glanced up at the tall, beefy vampire who smirked and winked at me and then looked to Allister who seemed a bit eager for me to join them as well. Sighing, I dropped my head. "Fine, but that's it. Unlike you, I have to sleep at night." I glanced at the watch on Allister's arm. "It's already nine o'clock."

"There's a good girl."

I jerked my arm out of Drake's arm and shoved him away. "I'm not a dog. Don't treat me like one." Placing both hands on Allister's arm, I gave him a squeeze and a smile. "You're the only gentleman in the whole household, I swear."

Drake barked out a laugh. "Allister, a gentleman?"

Allister's arm shot out and his brother in the shoulder shoving him into the brick wall of the restaurant. Rayne stopped talking to the hostess long enough to snap at us. "Stop screwing around and get in here."

While Drake continued to chuckle behind us, Allister led me to the table Rayne had acquired for us. Releasing my arm, he pulled my chair out for me. I smiled in thanks and sat down.

Picking up the menu, I glanced down at the prices. Wow. Fifty dollars for a salad. I peeked up from my menu to scan the room. Everyone was dressed really nice, suit jackets and cocktail dresses. The guys might have been able to pull off being in here with their expensive jeans and collared shirts, but I didn't think my outfit cost more than twenty dollars altogether including my underwear.

"How'd you get us a table?" I whispered to Rayne over my menu. "We're not exactly dressed for this place."

Rayne didn't look up from his menu. "They know us."

"Master Durands, a pleasure to have you in our little restaurant." An older man wearing a suit came to our table, his hands clasped together in front of him. He had the air of someone who was in charge. Maybe the manager? His eyes landed on me, and his beaming smile never faltered. "And who might this gorgeous young woman be?"

"Piper Billings." I offered him my hand to shake, but he bent over it, kissing it like some kind of Victorian gentleman. Oh-kay.

"I am Richard Griffin, the manager of this esteemed establishment. Any friend of the Durands is a friend of ours. Please, do not hesitate to ask for anything." To the others, he asked, "Would you like your usual?"

Drake and Allister nodded, handing over their menus, but Rayne held his hand up. "No, I want the Melanzana alla Parmigiana and a nice Sangiovese. Just bring the bottle. Please give Miss Billings the same thing."

Richard took Rayne's word for it and didn't even ask my opinion before he took the remaining menus and disappeared into the back. My jaw clenched, and I prepared to ream into him, but a waitress came next, giving us water and a plate of bread. I jiggled my foot and gripped my knife in my hand, waiting for her to stop eying the guys and leave. Not that they were doing a good job of getting rid of her as Drake kept asking her questions.

When she finally left, I picked my knife up and pointed it at Rayne. "I am not your pet. I can order my own food."

"We both know you can't afford this place—" Rayne started.

"That's beside the point."

"So, you should trust me to pick something you will like. I am paying after all." He paused as another waiter came out and poured the wine. Rayne swirled it around and gave it a sniff before sipping it. He nodded, and the waiter poured for everyone at the table.

Ignoring the glass, as soon as the waiter left, I snapped, "I didn't ask to come here. I can buy my own food or just eat at home. Stop treating me like some kind of doll you can dress up and feed whatever you want."

I expected Drake or at least Allister to jump in and help me out, but both of them were more than content to sit back and watch us snipe at each other. Freaking traitors.

"As far as I'm concerned, you are that," Rayne began but then held his hand up to stop me from arguing. "However, Antoine wants us to get along. To put our unpleasantness behind us. So... maybe, for a moment, you can stop finding reasons to hate me and take this meal and the clothes as a peace offering."

If this were a cartoon, my jaw would have hit the table. "A peace offering? Hate you? You're the one who has had it in for me since day one."

"That's true," Drake pointed out helpfully, earning him a look from Rayne. "What? It is."

"Fine," Rayne conceded. "We are both at fault, but this is our chance to remedy it before the party tomorrow. You don't want to show any weakness in front of these people. *We* can't afford to show any weakness, and you are a weakness."

"I am not."

"A little help here?" Rayne took a drink from his glass, no longer willing to argue with me.

I stared hard at the twins, daring them to tell me I was wrong. Allister avoided my gaze, picking his own wine glass up and busying himself with it.

Drake had no such issues. "You're unpredictable and undisciplined. Which we like," Drake added quickly, "but will make us look bad to the other masters."

"Masters?" I paused. "Who exactly is coming to this party?"

"Several of our fellow brothers." Drake's eyes moved around the table, looking for someone to add to it.

Something about the way he said it made me think of something. "Hold on a moment. I thought you guys were brothers, but you're not, are you?"

"Not in the traditional sense," Drake answered.

Allister added, "We are blood brothers."

"We all have the same sire or maker, whatever you want to call it." Rayne tapped his fingertips on the table, impatient to get on with it. "Every once in a while, he, our maker, decides to send one of his other... children to check up on the different factions."

"The Durands being the main one here," Drake continued for Rayne. "However, the person they're sending..."

"Valentine," Allister interjected with a displeased frown.

"... likes pretty women, especially unbroken ones."

My pulse pounded in my veins at Rayne's words. "Oh."

"Yes, oh."

Shaking my head and forcing myself to breathe, I asked, "Then why not hide me away? Why make a show of me being there at all?"

"Because if there is one thing our kind likes more than anything, it's taking other people's toys." Drake's lips curled up in a fiend grin. "If we hide you, then he will think you are important. If we put you on display..."

"He'll ignore me," I squeaked.

"That is our hope," Drake agreed.

"At least that's what Antoine has us believing," Rayne gave me a cruel grin. "It could just as easily be because he wants to taunt Valentine with what we have that he doesn't... which, in this case, would be you."

CHAPTER 27

Piper

THE DAY OF THE party didn't make the outfit any better. I stared at it on its hanger, and the dubious black frilly monstrosity that even an anime character would have scoffed at stared back with just as much contempt if not more.

Really, how much lower could I get?

I already cleaned their toilets, did their laundry, and made their beds. I mean, they were relatively clean, but still, I was waiting for that proverbial used condom to drop or at least a stiff wash rag to appear. They were guys after all. From my experience with them, vampires wanted sex just as much as the next hormonal driven Neanderthal.

Sighing, I chewed on my thumbnail while I hyped myself up to wear the damn thing. It wasn't that bad. It could be worse. They could make me wear something like this every day while cleaning the toilets, doing the laundry, and making their beds.

"Fuck, Piper, grow some balls." I threw my hands in the air and grabbed the thing off the hanger. I'd already put on the frilly underwear over my own. I opted out for a bra because the corset top pretty much kept the girls in place without any chances of a nip slip.

I got the dress on and halfway laced up when I remembered the shop lady had to help me get the rest of it done up before.

Crap.

Just as I start to panic, Darren knocked on the door. I knew it was him because he always knocked three times, soft but firm, before waiting a moment and then doing it again. He didn't yell or ask if I was there, not until I answered first. I wasn't sure if this was something the masters had instilled in him or if he decided to do it on his own. Either way, I was happy for the regularity.

"Come in, Darren, it's unlocked."

The doorknob turned, and Darren slipped in with a frown marring his lips. "You should never just assume a person is who they are or keep your door unlocked." His eyes moved to my partially dressed self. "Especially, while dressing."

I tapped my foot, my hands on my hips. "Sure, great. Got it. Now, will you help me lace up this blatant disrespect for feminism everywhere?" I spun around and gestured at the ties.

"Very well." Darren moved in behind me and tugged on the laces. "You should be grateful to be even included in tonight's events."

"Oh, should I?" I grunted, wincing as he pulled it tighter than the shop lady.

"Yes." Darren paused in his tugs for a moment. "Master Durand allowing you to come shows that he trusts you."

I snorted. "Not from what Rayne told me."

He jerked on the laces, making me groan. "Master Rayne. You should get into the habit of saying it now. If you slip up in front of the others tonight, you won't be happy with the outcome. Now, I wouldn't regard what Master Rayne says on one matter or the other."

"Why do you call him Master Rayne and then Antoine and Wynn Master Durand?"

"How else do I separate them when talking about them? If I called them all Durand, then it would be confusing, wouldn't it? However, if you want to be technical, Antoine is the only true Durand.

The rest of them took on his name when they decided to join his faction."

When he finished tying the corset, I smoothed my hands down the front and shifted from side to side. It didn't give a lot of freedom for movement. I'd be lucky if my penchant for knocking things over didn't come out like a vengeance tonight. The limited movement and heels were just asking for something to break.

"Here." Darren handed me something. It was a cloth hat on a headband, kind of like those maids wore before it turned into a kink. I gave him a look. "Don't ask me. I am a lowly servant, same as you."

I rolled my eyes. "Sure, you are."

Sighing, I turned back to the mirror and fixed the hat on my head. I'd taken the time to curl my hair, so fat curls fell over my shoulders to further cover my bare shoulders. I'd even gone so far as to apply some makeup. I told myself I was primping for the visitors so they wouldn't think badly of the masters, but really, I wanted to look good for Wynn. If this didn't make him want to jump my bones, I didn't know what would.

Moving over to the chair of my vanity, I sat down and went to work on pulling my stockings on. "So, what are the rules?"

"Rules?"

"You know, what can I and can't I do tonight?" I finished with one thigh high and went to grab the other one.

Darren picked up my romance novel from my side table and flipped through the pages. His brows raised as he no doubt realized it was a vampire romance novel before answering me.

"The usual rules apply. Be quiet unless spoken to. Try your best to not cause a disturbance." He moved his gaze over to me with a small, condescending smile. "We all know how hard that is for you but do try."

I scowled, grabbing my shoe. "I don't do it on purpose. I'm cursed. I can't help that the carpet moves or things are not in the place they were in before." I muttered and cursed as I fought with the buckle of my shoe. Freaking thing was worse than the corset.

"Of course, it isn't." Darren snapped the book shut and moved over to my side. He knelt and took the shoes from me. Buckling them with nimble fingers, he had both shoes on my feet before I could blink. "Cursed or not, you do have a penchant for opening your mouth when you should be silent."

Standing, I fluffed my skirt. "I do not. Okay, maybe a little bit, but they antagonize me. I'm not just going to sit back and take it."

"In this case, you should not only take it, but bend over and ask them to fuck you please."

I gaped at Darren's retreating back, not only at the use of language, something I'd never heard from him, but the instructions. He might be able to just deal with it, but I was not in the habit of laying back and thinking of England. I'd sooner take a stake to bed than let those self-imposing leeches walk all over me.

Quickly following Darren into the hallway and down the stairs, I waited at the front door. He had his own outfit, well, if you call a traditional butler suit with white gloves an outfit. It wasn't much different than I saw him wear on a regular basis. Maybe the suit was a bit more expensive, and his hair was more carefully slicked back, but really, he looked pretty much the same.

"We wait here until the guests arrive," Darren instructed, pulling a pocket watch, yes, a goddamn pocket watch, from his vest pocket. "Which should be any moment now. Then the masters will come in, and we will take any coats they have."

"Coats?" I rocked on my heels, trying to break them in faster. I was going to have blisters on my feet by the end of the night, I was sure. "Do vampires even feel the cold?"

Not missing a beat, Darren told me, "Appearances... and stop fidgeting." He grabbed my arm, and I stopped. Releasing me, he laced his hands behind his back and continued. "The guests will then be ushered to the drawing room for pre-dinner drinks."

"Wait, are we talking alcohol or…?"

"Whatever the guests want," Darren snapped, clearly getting impatient with my interruptions. "Then there is dinner, and hopefully, if everything goes off without a hitch," he gave me a pointed look, "they will leave, and we can all go back to our regular lives."

Straightening my back, I nodded. "Sounds good."

We waited in the foyer for a good twenty minutes without anyone coming. I started to get antsy, tugging on my skirt and then wiggling my rib cage from side to side.

"Stop it," Darren hissed, his eyes jerking to me. "Be still."

"Easy for you to say, you're not bound and fluffed up like an overdressed peacock." I reached beneath my skirt and pulled at the frilly underwear which had ridden up my butt crack.

"Piper," Wynn's voice called out, making me freeze.

Of course, he'd come right when I was picking a wedgie. Jerking my hand out of my skirt and cupping my hands in front of me, I turned to smile at him. Wynn descended from the stairs cloaked in a dark plume shirt and black dress slacks, looking as delicious as ever. His ebony hair was still damp from his shower and curled at his neckline.

"Wy- I mean, Master Durand," I caught myself and curtsied. "You are looking handsome tonight."

"Thank you. I have to say you are looking ravishing tonight yourself." His eyes trailed over my outfit, and a flash of hunger crossed over his face. I'd have to thank Rayne later. I guess all men, vampire or not, had a maid kink.

"Master Durand." Darren stepped forward, a stern frown on his face. "The guests have not arrived—" The doorbell rang out through the house, cutting Darren off. "Never mind. It seems they are here. Excuse me."

Darren took the few steps to the door and pulled it open without looking at who it was behind it. Not waiting to greet them, he opened the door completely and waited beside it for the guests to come in. "Welcome, we shall start with drinks in the drawing room. Please hand your coats to Piper, she will be happy to take care of them for you."

Wynn gave me a small, encouraging smile before heading into the drawing room. My head moved from him to the door where one of the most beautiful men I'd ever laid eyes on entered. I mean, really, he could give Wynn and the others a run for their money.

Light brown hair curled on the top of his head, the sides buzzed but with enough stubble to melt into the scruff on his chin and cheeks. Pulling his jacket off, he tossed it in my direction. I caught it even though I was taking in the pin striped suit that clung to his swimmer body form. His milk chocolate eyes skimmed over me briefly before turning away.

Not bothered by his dismissal, I took the jacket and laid it over my arm.

"Valentine Moretti," Antoine exclaimed, moving down the stairs in a slow and graceful stride. "How wonderful to see you again."

"What's it been? Fifty years?" Valentine grinned, but the smile was not a pleasant one. It made my stomach twist into knots for some reason I couldn't describe.

"Forty-six, but who's counting?" Antoine gave Valentine a tight smile, obviously no happier for him to be here than Valentine. Just as I thought they might go into the drawing room, a breathtaking woman entered.

Long black hair fell down her back in waves of curls, just stopping at the swell of her butt. She flung her fur coat in my direction without so much as a how do you do, revealing a silver, tight-fitted silk gown that looked more like a nightgown than something you'd wear to a party. Her heels were spiked and at least four inches tall. I'd have fallen on my face wearing them.

"I can't believe you made me take a cab," the woman griped, holding the matching silver clutch in her hand. "I could smell the driver all the way in the back seat. I'd have eaten him, but I fear he'd rub his disgusting scent all over me."

"Theresa." Antoine nodded to the woman, not once looking in my direction. "Looking as lovely as ever."

Theresa flipped her hair, even though it did not need flipping, and gave him a sultry smile. "And you're just as stiff as ever. Where's your brother? Where's my Wynn?"

I stiffened. Her Wynn? I suddenly had the urge to burn the woman's coat in my hands. My fingers curled around the fabric, twisting it beneath my hands as I watched them walking into the drawing room.

"Breathe, Piper." Darren reminded me, taking the coats from my hands and laying them across the stair's railing. "If you can't handle a few snide comments, then you won't last the night."

I forced myself to relax, wiggling some of the tension out before looking to Darren. "Better?"

"Much, now for the drinks." Darren inclined his head toward the drawing room. "You find out what they want, and I'll prepare them. Then you can bring them back out. Think you can handle that?"

I swallowed thickly, my heart racing in my chest. "Yes. I think so."

"Good. Now, come, before they start getting antsy. A hungry vampire is never a pretty sight."

Following closely after Darren and into the drawing room, I kept my eyes down but peeked around me as I passed by. Wynn sat on one of the tall back chairs, one leg crossed over the other and a pleasant expression on his face. I wanted to think he was trying not to throw Theresa, who had taken up residence on the arm of his chair out the window. She was pawing him like she owned him, her hands dipping into the open neck of his shirt and her mouth skimming his ear.

I was watching them so closely that I almost tripped and fell into Rayne's lap. I caught myself at the last moment, my hand on the back of his chair. I muttered an apology before hurrying after Darren.

The twins sat side by side on one of the couches with Antoine on the opposite one. Marcus stood behind and off to the side of Antoine's chair, his arms crossed over his chest. His dark eyes scanned the room as if he expected trouble at any moment.

Valentine had taken a seat next to Antoine though it seemed neither of them wanted to be there. It made me wonder what the point of tonight was if none of them like each other.

"Gentlemen and lady," Darren addressed the room, nodding toward Theresa. "Please let Piper know what you would like to drink. We have all manner of alcohol as well as several blood types on hand."

All eyes locked onto me as Darren finished, and I stood there frozen for a second. It took Darren giving me a discrete shove forward before I started moving. Deciding it best to start with the guests, I stopped beside Valentine.

"What can I get you, Master Moretti?" I surprised myself by how demure my voice came out as I kept my eyes down to not show how freaked out I felt.

"Aw, look at this one. So precious. She's shaking. Please, pet, call me Valentine." He chuckled as I nodded. "I'll take red wine mixed with AB positive. You still have some, don't you, Antoine?"

"Of course." Antoine's voice came out clipped but courteous. At least one of us was good at hiding our feelings.

I went around the room and took the drink orders, feeling more and more discouraged when none of the brothers gave me a passing glance. In fact, it seemed like they were trying their best to ignore me altogether.

"How are you holding up?" Darren asked when I came into the kitchen with their orders. He began to fill them as I tapped my fingers on the counter.

"Okay, I guess. Nervous."

"As I would expect. Just keep your mouth shut and your head down unless spoken to otherwise and you'll be fine." He began to fill a silver tray for me and then added, "I wouldn't listen too closely to what they talk about. Better not to listen to them at all. Think of yourself as one of those Queen's guards in England."

I licked my lips and tried to think like them. Really, it couldn't be that hard. Think tall, reserved, a big fuzzy head. Okay, not that far. I could do this.

Keeping to my mantra, I made it through the first round of drinks before I had a reason to break my character. I mean, it was a good reason. I couldn't really be blamed for what I did. Valentine more than deserved it.

A bit drunk on wine and blood, the vampire turned their discussion from work to more personal matters.

"So, tell me, Antoine. Does this one taste as good as she looks?" Valentine flashed me his fangs, clear hunger in his eyes. He didn't wait for Antoine to answer before continuing to cut me down like a piece of steak he was perusing over at the supermarket. "Is she a virgin? You know virgin blood is the sweetest of them all." Valentine kissed his fingers in my direction.

I regretted my decision to stand there within arm's reach of this disgusting creature. Pluto wouldn't be far enough away from him. My hand tightened around the silver tray, and my horrified expression landed on Antoine who didn't so much as blink an eye.

"Come now, Valentine. We all know Italian nuns are the best," Wynn announced with a jovial laugh, causing the other vampire to glance his way and thankfully taking his putrid gaze off me.

"You aren't wrong." The visiting vampire chuckled, but then he moved back to me. "However, Italians are so protective of their convents as of late. I remember the days where you could walk into any church and with a bit of charm here and a cut throat there, you could be drinking nun for the month." He leered at me, his hand reaching out to tug on my skirt. "This one, however, is much too pretty to be a nun or a virgin really. Come on, darling, tell me. Do you like it rough?"

Unable to hold back any longer and since my employers, all fucking six of them, seemed to have forgotten how to speak at that moment, I had to take matters into my own hands. Giving him a nasty grin, I snarled, "If you wanted a stake to your heart, you only had to ask, Master Valentine."

The room quieted. Visible tension could be cut like a knife, and for a moment, I worried for my life. Then the woman, the dark-haired beauty hanging all over Wynn jerked a finger in my direction.

"Are you going to let her talk to him that way?"

I glared at her, wanting nothing more than to throw my tray at her head. Hopefully, it would cut her pretty little head off, silence her and still those roaming hands of hers for good.

The twins stayed where they were, looking imposing and ready to jump up in case a fight did break out. Though I doubted they could reach me in time if Valentine decided to take his anger out on me.

Rayne was the only one who surprised me. Unlike his older brother, Antoine, who had done nothing but sit with a bored expression on his face, not being more useful than a statue, to be honest, Rayne's eyes bore into Valentine. I couldn't figure out if the fiery hatred in his eyes were for my sake or just the vampire himself. Either could have been valid.

Valentine, however, didn't react the way his companion did. He stared at me for a moment as if unsure he had heard me right, and then threw his head back and laughed.

It was a sound that ran through me and made me ill.

"It's quite alright, Theresa. I like my women with a bit of sass. It makes them taste all the better. I do so like a good fight." His eyes zeroed in on me with a cruel grin, and I'd had it.

With a liquefying look around the room, I spun on my heels and stomped from the room. Antoine called after me, but I ignored him and the laughter trailing after me. Fuck them. Fuck them all.

CHAPTER 28

Drake

FUCK, WHAT A DRAG. I'd rather have my fangs pulled out with pliers than sit there and listen to Valentine and Theresa brag about how lovely it was at the main house.

Screw them.

They seemed to forget that we lived at the main house for years, and we left as soon as we had the chance. Being in a large house full of vampires like them who didn't care for human life like we did made you forget your humanity over the years.

It was easy to think you aren't losing it when everyone around you was acting worse... or even egging you on.

Valentine was the worst of the instigators. Valentine loved to find virgins, sometimes not even old enough to have bled yet, and spend his time breaking them in before tossing them to someone else if he didn't kill them first.

Theresa wasn't any better.

When she wasn't trying to jump on Wynn's dick, she liked to cause pain in the most unusual manners. I remembered a time she had used a feather duster to bring a man to the point of orgasm and then killed him with it midway through.

The very thought of it made me wince.

"Stop with the walk down memory lane," Rayne growled lowly, crossing one leg over the other as he grimaced.

"Sorry," I muttered, darting my eyes away from him and back to the vampire guests. They didn't care about the rest of us, only Wynn and Antoine. In most cases, I wouldn't care. Better them than me.

However, Valentine had already crossed a line with Piper.

Rage had been simmering inside me ever since his beady gaze trailed over her skin. I wanted to pluck his eyes from his head and shove them down his throat for even thinking of touching her. Then he had the audacity to put his hands on her and even went so far as to treat her like she wasn't a person. These were the kinds of people we had to deal with at the main house.

"The visual isn't helping either," Rayne reminded me, running a hand through his hair, his teeth tightly clenched.

I was about to apologize again, but a nasally voice stopped me.

"Wynn," Theresa whined, her hands pulling at his shirt as she was still trying to undress him right there, "why don't we go find somewhere a bit quieter? I've missed you."

Allister snorted.

"What?" Theresa snapped, her eyes jerking up from Wynn.

"I don't see why you need a room. It's not like you've needed one before," Allister reminded her with a disgusted growl.

"Allister."

Antoine's warning tone made my brother clamp his mouth shut, but he didn't tear his glare away from the piece of trash who called herself a lady.

"It's good to see you haven't lost your handle on your boys." Theresa let a sly grin slide over her face as she snuggled into Wynn even further. The poor bastard just took in stride, but I knew him well enough to see the tick by his eye brow. If holy water worked on us, he'd be bathing in it right after this.

"They are hardly boys," Antoine reminded her, leaning on the arm of the couch. One would think it was a natural position, but it was most likely to keep as far away as possible from Valentine as he could.

Theresa's eyes dipped down to Wynn, her tongue sneaking out to wet her lips. "That they are not."

Ugh. Fuck me with a blunt stake. I envied Piper a bit. I wished I could stomp out of here because I was offended.

"Ditto," Rayne muttered, shifting uncomfortably in his seat.

"Where did that lovely maid of yours run off to?" Valentine asked, his eyes moved around the room far too eager to find a victim to sink his teeth into.

"Working elsewhere," Antoine bit out.

As if waiting for the mention of her, Darren came into the drawing room. "Dinner is ready if you would follow me."

Valentine stood with the rest of us, but as we moved into the dining room and took our seats, I noticed he didn't enter with us.

"Rayne," I grabbed his arm, "Valentine is missing. Can you hear him?"

The redhead stopped and frowned, his eyes moving to the ceiling for a moment. Then his eyes widened, and he was gone before I could ask him what he had heard.

"Where'd Rayne go?" Allister asked as I took my seat beside him.

Picking up my knife and tapping the bottom of it on the table with my anxiety growing, I shook my head. "I don't know. Trouble."

"Fuck." Allister mimicked my head shake. "And here I thought we might get out of this without bloodshed."

I chuckled at that. "We're vampires. If there's not a bit of blood spilled, it isn't a party."

Sighing with a sad smile, Allister leaned back in his seat. "Too true."

I watched the others, waiting to see when Antoine would notice. When he did, he didn't get up. He didn't freak out or even stand up. Antoine, ever the calm and poised one, gestured to Darren.

Darren leaned down next to him, his mouth close to Antoine's ear. The human servant had learned to speak low enough that no one but Antoine's could hear him, and what he said made Antoine's lip tick.

With a jerk of his head, Antoine sent Darren on his way. Dinner started as if two of the party weren't missing and the maid wasn't in peril.

Who could eat at a time like this?

CHAPTER 29

Piper

I RUSHED OUT OF the room, my face flaming and heart pounding. I ignored Darren's curious eyes and kept my head down as I fast walked through the kitchen.

Running upstairs, I darted into my room, shutting and locking the door behind me. I paced back and forth before my bed, my arms wrapped around myself. The sound of their laughter still echoed in my ears. I shook my head to clear it, but it didn't work. Moving over to my bed, I found my phone and pulled up my playlist. I plugged my headphones in and blared music in my ears until I couldn't hear them anymore.

I didn't care if I never heard again or if my eardrums burst as long as I never had to hear Valentine's creepy laughter ever again. After a few moments, my head and ears hurt enough that I turned the music off. Chucking my phone onto my bed, I started pacing again, this time a bit more forcefully. My fear had fettered out, and anger replaced it, making me snarl and curse.

If this was Antoine trusting me, then I didn't want any part of it. I'd rather be kept in the dark and safely hidden behind my locked door than in that room with those monsters. How could he, how could they, just sit there and let them talk about me that way?

"A delicacy, my ass," I muttered to myself, getting even madder by the minute. I caught sight of my reflection in the mirror and snagged the hat off my head, crumpling it up in my hand before throwing it down. "Fuck you, Valentine. Fuck Antoine. Fuck Rayne." I stomped my feet with each name, getting more aggressive as I went. "Fuck the twins and specifically fuck Wynn. Fuck. Fuck. Fuck!"

Of all of them, I'd thought Wynn would have come to my aid. He was supposed to be a gentleman, and on top of that, we were blood bonded now for however long that lasted. Wynn should have been the first person to stand up for me, to knock Valentine's overly white fangs out.

I shuddered, my hand clinging to my shoulders.

There was not enough money in the world to ever get me to work in that monster's house. Even if I didn't already know about his kink, five minutes with him told me I'd be dead by the end of the day.

I dragged my hands through my hair, not caring if I messed up my curls and then flopped down on the ground. Glaring at the door, I slumped over, my hands falling to either side of me. I felt like a broken wind-up doll, waiting for someone to come and crank me back up. I probably looked it as well.

Would I get fired if I didn't go back down there? Would they even notice I'm gone? Darren sure noticed, but he had yet to make an appearance to drag me back to the party.

"Probably too busy kissing ass to care," I grumbled, crossing my arms over my chest and beating my feet against the ground for good measure. If I was going to throw a fit, I might as well get it all out now.

After a good five minutes, I took a deep breath, held it, before letting it out all in one go. Standing, I fluffed my dress and searched for my hat. Grimacing at the wrinkled contraption, I tried to smooth it out as best as I could before putting it back on my head.

I turned to the mirror and sighed. A bit disheveled but it'd have to do.

Heading for the door, I muttered to myself, "One more word, I swear. One more question about my virginal status and I'm going to smack someone. Preferably Valentine."

Throwing the door open, I walked out the door and right into a hard chest. Quickly shutting the door behind me, I moved away from them, muttering an apology. I half bowed for good measure.

"No apology needed."

At the sound of the voice, my eyes moved up the brass buttons of the pin striped vest and over the sharp chin with a dusting of scruff before locking with light brown eyes crinkled in amusement. Realizing who he was, I jerked my eyes down to his nose.

"Why, hello, Piper. Fancy meeting you here." Valentine's smooth voice, no doubt meant to be seductive and perhaps calming, only made my apprehension rise.

I took a step back from him, reaching for the door handle of my room. Then, realizing I was giving him an option to get me cornered, I released the doorknob and cleared my throat. "Hello, Master Valentine. Can I help you with something?"

"Your name is Piper, correct?" One hand was tucked into his pocket while the other one reached out and touched the ends of my hair.

I forced myself not to move. If I didn't antagonize him, then he would get bored and move on. Giving him my best demure look, I placed one hand over the other and nodded. "Yes. That is correct. Can I be of some assistance?"

Valentine frowned at my tone, and I snickered on the inside. Thought you could catch me off guard, did you? I showed you. Go fall on a stake, you sick fuck.

"Why so shy? You were so forthcoming downstairs." Valentine took a step toward me, a smirk on his lips. He was in on my game. "Don't tell me it was for show? Maybe you wanted one of the Durands to come to the rescue? Is that it?"

I smiled even brighter, my fingers curling into my hands until the nails bit into my skin. "Of course not, Master Valentine. I apologize for my earlier behavior. I am still new to your world."

His smirk slipped a bit, but then he moved even closer until he was just a hair's breadth away. "Please, call me Valentine. All this master nonsense is so old-fashioned. I'm a modern vampire myself." His other hand touched my shoulder, and I fought the need to tense up.

"As you wish." I beamed and then took a step away from him. "If you'll excuse me, I must return to the party before I am missed."

I didn't get more than two steps down the hall before Valentine's hand latched onto my elbow and jerked me around. Slamming me into his front, his arm locked around my middle like a vice, giving me no chance to escape.

"Come now, don't leave so soon. We are just getting to know each other." His words came out as a purr, but there was a sharpness to his voice. I kept my eyes on his throat, refusing to be taken over by his vampire charms.

"I really should get going. Please release me." I tried my best to keep an even tone and not freak out. No need to excite him further.

Unfortunately, I wasn't fully in control of my body and so I stiffened as his head lowered. His nose buried in my hair, and he inhaled deeply, a low rumble vibrating through him. I swore I felt something poking me in the stomach.

"Such a pretty little thing. Too bad your owners don't know the value of someone like you, the immeasurable amount of pleasure you could give them."

I swallowed hard and squeezed my eyes shut. "I'm sure you're mistaken. I'm not all that remarkable. Just a plain old maid. Nothing more."

Valentine chuckled and lifted his head, much to my relief. "I'm sure your unappreciative masters have filled your head with such nonsense, but I think I should be the judge of that." Quicker than I could follow, his hand grabbed hold of the lace collar around my neck and jerked it off. The fabric ripped, and I gasped.

He wasn't going to bite me, was he?

One moment, I was in Valentine's embrace, and the next, I was clutched against a familiar chest. With one hand in my hair and the other on my sternum, Rayne's fingers brushed the curve of my breasts as he held my back tightly against his front.

"Valentine. What are you doing to my maid?" The possessive tone in his voice in usual circumstances would have pissed me off, but right now, I'd take it over Valentine any day.

Valentine's eyes widened a fraction, but then a cool blank expression covered his face. Crossing one arm under the other, he acted like Rayne had simply asked him the time of day. "Nothing for circumstance. She is not claimed. I figured I could take her off your hands."

Claimed? I bristled at the words, but Rayne's hand in my hair tightened, warning me to stay quiet. Pinching my lips closed, I lowered my eyes to the ground, forcing myself to act the dutiful servant. God, Rayne was so going to get his when this was all over.

"What makes you think that?" Rayne pressed me closer, his hand moving lower until it settled on my stomach. Against my better judgment, my body reacted to his hands on me. I shifted my legs and took a few shallow breaths. Remember, asshole. Asshole. A chauvinistic pompous assho—

"I don't see any marks." Valentine waved a hand in my direction, and I stopped thinking about how Rayne affected me. Did he mean bite marks? There was no way I was schooling my features for that one.

Rayne, however, seemed to be more than prepared for Valentine's inquiries. He pressed his cheek to the side of my head as a condescending tone filled his voice. "Not everyone goes straight for the jugular, Valentine. There are far more delicious places to mark one's own."

God, fuck. Where had that come from? When did the little, redheaded shit learn to seduce like that? He wasn't even trying to turn me on, and I was ready to collapse on my wobbly knees.

Valentine made a noise in the back of his throat, clearly not believing Rayne. I didn't know why, I know I sure did.

Rayne figured the same because the hand in my hair whipped my head back and his mouth captured mine. A startled sound came from me, but he swallowed it whole. His tongue assaulted my mouth, dragging my own tongue into his hot cavern. My hands which had been dead at my sides now clutched at his hand on my stomach, my eyes squeezing shut, but I didn't push him away.

It was for Valentine's sake, of course, not because Rayne kissed like he was fucking my mouth, leaving me thoroughly breathless and aching by the time he released my mouth. But not before his fang nipped my lip, causing a trail of blood to drip down my chin.

Not meeting my eyes, Rayne licked the blood from my face, teasing the corner of my lips before releasing me completely.

Still not looking at me directly, Rayne turned his gaze back to Valentine. "Satisfied?"

Valentine huffed, a mixture of disappointment and annoyance in that one sound. "Fine. Then find me something else to eat, I'm going to starve in this house." He spun on his heel and started back for the stairs, only giving me a passing glance over his shoulder as he left.

When Valentine's footsteps sounded on the stairs, I turned to Rayne, opening my mouth to ask him what the fuck that was, but he shook his head, his eyes staring at the place Valentine had been. "Go wait in my room, Piper. I'll be there shortly."

Opening and shutting my mouth like a gaping fish, I began to argue, but then Rayne's eyes pivoted to mine. There was something in his amber eyes, a warning of some kind that had me swallowing my complaints.

My head bobbed, and I shifted away from him on unsteady legs. "Of course, Master Durand."

I walked on stiffening legs to his room, my eyes forward and telling myself not to look back no matter how much I wanted to. Rayne had saved me from Valentine's clutches, but was I really truly safe?

Safe inside of his bedroom, I took my shoes off before climbing onto his bed. There wasn't anywhere else to sit, and I wasn't going to sit on the floor. Who knew how long it would take him to show up?

I should have taken that other job. Vampires. Blood bonds. Hot sexy males that have no sense of personal boundaries. Okay, so maybe it went both ways, and maybe it was only a couple of them, but still, I wouldn't have any of these problems if I had taken the call center job before I had joined the temp agency.

I sat on his bed, my arms around my knees for hours. Rayne never came. I didn't know when I fell asleep, but when I woke, the sun had risen, and someone had covered me with a blanket. I glanced around the room. There was no Rayne or anyone else in sight, no sign that anyone had come in beside the blanket.

Climbing out of the bed, I folded the blanket and placed it on the bed before heading for the door. I hadn't locked it, not knowing if Rayne would be able to get in. It was his room after all.

Once the door was opened, I wasn't sure I wanted to leave. Were they gone? Had Valentine and his whole horrible crew left? Did I want to chance it?

Peeking my head out, I searched for some sign of the visiting vampires, but as the sun was up, I wasn't surprised to find the hallways empty.

Not leaving it to chance, I ran out of Rayne's room and down the hallway. I stopped briefly at the balcony overlooking the foyer. No sign of any of them. Even the coats from last night had been picked up off the stair railing.

Heaving out a shaky breath, I moved with more confidence to my room. Once inside, I locked the door tight and went about taking last night's outfit off. If I never had to wear it again, it would be too soon. Resisting the urge to burn it, I sat it on the nearby chair and climbed into the tub.

Turning the water on scalding, I scrubbed at my skin. I could still feel Valentine's hands on me. The sickly-sweet scent of his aftershave clung to my form. Even Rayne's spicy scent didn't cover Valentine's.

At the thought of Rayne, my fingers went to my lips. What had he been thinking? What had I been thinking about letting him?

Even more than the chilling charms of Valentine, I remembered Rayne's possessive hands on my body. His mouth claiming mine. The copper taste of my blood tainting our kiss. Remembering it made me shiver even though the water was so hot that it could burn the flesh from my bones.

I stayed in the shower until the water ran cold and then climbed out. Barely taking the time to dry myself off, I climbed into my bed and drew the covers around me. As my eyes fluttered closed once more, I realized one scary fact.

For all of Rayne's faults, I'd liked that kiss.

CHAPTER 30

Piper

AFTER THE PARTY, THINGS pretty much went back to normal. Wynn and I flirted around each other, neither one of us daring to take it any further. While in my bedroom, I pretended he was mine.

However, my daydreams had started to shift. It wasn't just Wynn who whispered sweet nothings to me. More and more, my mind shifted back to that kiss in the hallway with Rayne. I couldn't get it off my mind or the redhead in question, though I couldn't say the same for him.

If anything, instead of annoying me beyond measure, Rayne had been avoiding me. If I entered a room, he left it. If I was in a room, he turned back around even if what he wanted was in the same room I was in. It was getting ridiculous.

"What are we, high schoolers?" I muttered to myself as I watched his back retreating from me once more. I had just sat down for dinner when Rayne had come in for his nightly ration of blood. His amber eyes locked with mine, and for a moment I thought he might stay, maybe talk to me, but then he swallowed visibly and fled the room.

"Master Rayne seems more distracted than usual," Gretchen commented from the seat next to me. "Did something happen, perhaps?"

Licking my suddenly dry lips, I shook my head. I pulled my eyes away from where he had stood and back to my plate. "I wouldn't know. I'm just the help."

Gretchen snorted and exchanged a knowing look with Darren. The two of them knew the masters far better than I did, but if Rayne wasn't telling about our encounter last weekend, I wasn't going to be the one to do it.

"I hope you're being smart." Darren sat his plate down on the island on the other side of me and then slid into the seat. The warning in his eyes was clear, but I wasn't taking the bait.

"Of course," I snapped, stabbing at my food. "I do my job and go to bed. That's it."

"What about outside the house?" Gretchen asked, politely. "I'm sure a pretty girl like you has a string of heartbroken men out there just waiting for her to crook her finger their way."

I barked a laugh. "Sure. Let me just find some time between warding off visiting vampires and cleaning the toilets." I rolled my eyes.

"You had today off," Darren reminded me with a frown. "Why didn't you take that time to have a social life?"

Sighing, I pushed my plate away from me. My appetite had all but vanished. "Yeah, that'd be easy enough. And when they ask what I do for a living, what do I tell them? I don't think Master Durand would be too happy about my spreading his secrets to the masses."

Letting out an impatient sound, Darren folded his napkin in his lap. "You tell them you're a maid which you are."

"I think it would be healthy for you to find a friend outside of the house," Gretchen went on as if there were no elephant in the room keeping me from doing just that. "Preferably a male one." She winked at me, and I couldn't help but smile.

"Fine. Fine." I stood and pushed back my seat. "I'll find a boyfriend if that will keep you all happy and off my back. Perhaps you'd like a play by play of our relationship? Maybe a video and an invitation to the wedding?"

"A video is hardly necessary, but I wouldn't say no to a wedding invitation." Gretchen beamed at me.

"Who's getting married?" Drake asked, standing in the doorway of the kitchen.

"I am apparently," I halfheartedly announced, moving to the fridge for a drink. "You're all invited." Pulling out a bottle of water, I twisted the cap off and took a long refreshing drink.

"Oh good, Rayne finally stopped moping and asked you."

I sputtered and coughed, choking on the very water I had been drinking. "What?" I gaped at Drake's grinning face.

"Master Durand." Gretchen tut-tutted with a motherly grin, waved a finger at Drake. "You shouldn't kid about such thing. You'll give Piper a heart attack." She moved out of her seat and over to the pot. "Can I get you a plate?"

Drake shook his head, still grinning like a fiend. "Not today, trying to watch my weight." He patted his stomach, making me frown.

Did vampires get fat?

Continuing as if he hadn't just come into the kitchen to screw with me, Drake moved to the fridge and pulled out his container of blood. "I actually came here to tell Piper that Antoine is looking for you."

I groaned, and Drake chuckled over the lip of the cup.

Sitting my water bottle down, I walked toward the stairs. My shoulders slumped and my eyes on the floor. "If I'm not back in thirty minutes, buy me a ticket out of the country."

"For what?" Drake asked.

"For staking your brother," I muttered low enough that I thought they couldn't hear me, but Drake's laughter followed me up the stairs.

Sunday, my one day off, had turned into the day that Antoine liked to call me into his office and ream me about all the things I'd done wrong that week. Last week, he'd chewed me out for leaving the house a mess after the party. What did he want me to do, spend my whole day off cleaning up after them? I mean, I did that the previous week, he couldn't expect me to do it every weekend.

If so, I needed a new day off that didn't follow an event.

Walking as slow as possible, I scuffed my shoes against the ground. It always felt like I was being called to the principal's office which I wouldn't have minded had it involved more spankings and far less sneers coming from both of us. I really think Antoine just needed a really good fuck or at least a hand getting the stick out of his ass.

"He can be so charming when he wants to be," I reminded myself as I came to a stop before his office door. When I'd wanted to quit, he all but had me melting into his hands, but he only seemed to keep that charm as a last resort. "More flies with honey..."

"Are you going to stand out there all night?" Antoine's voice wafted through the office door, and I scowled at the closed door.

Finally opening the door, I stepped inside.

Antoine sat behind his large desk per usual, the top of it covered with mountains of paperwork. I didn't quite know what they did for money, but it obviously included lots of paperwork and the ability to sleep all day and party at night.

Maybe they had stocks from the 1920s?

"You wanted to see me?" I laced my fingers in front of me, choosing to try the polite approach first. He, like Rayne, had a way of rubbing me the wrong way. It was like they purposely sought to piss me off. However, it was more Antoine than Rayne lately since the latter was avoiding me.

Antoine's long blonde hair covered part of his face, the face that hadn't done the polite thing and acknowledge me. Even though he didn't leave the house, not as far as I could tell in any case, Antoine still wore suits that accented his form and did nothing to hide that lovely body beneath it.

Stop talking about him like you're ever going to get a chance to see it for yourself.

"I wanted to talk to you about an upsetting phone call I just had." Antoine's tone left no hint of what that phone call could have entailed or if he was actually upset by it.

"A phone call?"

"Yes, about you."

I didn't know who could have called him. Like Gretchen and Darren had pointed out, I didn't have a tangible social life outside of the household, nor had I spoken to anyone who would have called Antoine about me. My parents didn't call unless I did first. My brother was overseas still doing god knows what.

Shaking my head, I decided I couldn't think of anything pressing that could have caused Antoine to be upset with me. "What was it about?"

Antoine put his pen down and placed his hands on top of the desk. His pale eyes locked onto me, a low, burning anger rising in the depths of his gaze. He was mad. Why?

"I knew this would happen. I blame myself. You weren't ready to face the other vampires yet, and still, I pushed you to it." Antoine sighed and rubbed a hand over his face as if he weren't aching to yell at me.

"So, this is about last weekend?" I took a stab in the dark. "I already apologized. I can't make up for my behavior any more than I already have." Irritation itched at the back of my throat, and I refrained from raising my voice. Really? He couldn't expect me to grovel for the rest of my life.

"You were supposed to be silent, seen but not heard," Antoine started with a sharpness to his tone, "but that is an impossible feat for you, isn't it? You can't help but speak your mind."

I scowled. "I'm not in the habit of letting people walk all over me."

"Clearly," Antoine snapped, "and now Valentine has put in an offer for you."

"What?"

"He wants to buy you."

My brows scrunched together, and then my eyes widened. "What? He can't buy me. I'm not for sale."

"He doesn't see it that way." Antoine picked his pen back up and shifted a few papers.

"And you told him no, right?" When Antoine didn't answer immediately, I rushed for his desk, my hands curling around the edge of the desk. "Right?"

Letting out an agitated breath, Antoine dropped his pen. "Of course, I did. It was hard enough getting a decent maid, I couldn't very well give you up so easily."

"I'm so thrilled," I replied dryly.

"It's your own fault." He pointed a long finger at me. "You should have kept your mouth shut and done your job."

Why that arrogant mother fu—

"If you hadn't dressed me like some plaything, then maybe he wouldn't have noticed me," I shot back, slamming my hand on the desktop. "Don't think I don't know what you were doing. I'm not your pet you can use to torment the other vampires. I'm a human being, and you will treat me with the respect I deserve."

Antoine's jaw ticked. He pressed his fingers into a steeple and locked those pale blue eyes with mine. "You are an employee of this household. If I want to rub you in the face of our competitors, then I will do as such. You were never in any danger, so your complaints are not valid nor needed."

I opened my mouth to argue, but he beat me to it.

"Rayne told me what happened in the hallway, and you are lucky he was there to defuse the situation." Antoine picked up his pen and returned to scribbling on his paper.

"I wouldn't have been in that situation if it hadn't been for you." I pointed at him, pissed off that he'd dismissed me so easily. "My sexual status or lack thereof is none of your or your guest's business."

"Then perhaps you shouldn't moan so loudly while in your bedroom in a house full of vampires."

Antoine's knee jerking comment made my stomach plummet. I always kind of assumed they couldn't hear me. It's not like I was being loud. I was in a locked room for crying out loud. Or rather that's what got me into this mess in the first place.

"So, now, I'm supposed to be celibate as well as ridiculed?" I attempted to turn the conversation back to what really mattered, the fact that this was all his fault.

He paused in his writing to read over what he had written. "Your sexual escapades are none of my concern as you stated, as long as they are done out of this house and not with any of my brothers. However, if you are unable to refrain from scratching your itch on the premises, I suggest you practice orgasming without moaning like a dying cow."

I gaped at him.

When I didn't speak again for a moment, Antoine glanced up from his paper and shooed me with his pen. "If that's all, I have work to do."

Pure fury liquefied my inside and I grabbed the first thing I could get my hands on, a book in this case, and threw it at him. Of course, I never expected to hit him. Vampire reflexes and all. So, it was no surprise when Antoine shifted to one side just at the book sailed toward his face.

"Go find a stake and fall on it." I spun on my heel and stomped toward the door.

"Close it behind you."

Spinning back around, I grabbed the doorknob and yelled, "And I do not moan like a dying cow!" I slammed the door for good measure, half mortified and half wanting to burn the house down with Antoine stuck inside.

Marching down the stairs, I headed for the kitchen. It was my day off. I was going to eat comfort food, watch some T.V., and then rub one out just to spite him. "I'll show you who moans like a cow," I muttered as I jerked the fridge door open.

Darren, who was washing dishes, glanced up at me for a moment and then returned to his task. He was used to my temper tantrums by now, no doubt, and probably didn't want to get in the middle of it.

I grabbed a pint of ice cream and then a spoon from the drying rack by the sink and made for the stairs. Stupid vampires and their stupid heightened senses. A girl couldn't fantasize about her bosses in peace? What was the world coming to?

"Piper," Darren called to me, stopping my ascent upstairs. Turning around to face him, he pushed a vase full of white roses toward me. "These came for you."

Frowning, I climbed down the stairs and over to the island. With a curious little smile, I picked the vase up and sniffed the roses. A sickly-sweet scent filled my nose, making me sneeze.

"Who would be sending me flowers?"

Darren only shrugged and turned back to his dishes.

I plucked the card from the vase and opened it. As my eyes comprehended the words on the paper, the vase slipped from my hand and crashed to the floor. Glass shattered, the water and flowers decorated the pieces in an almost purposeful design.

Rushing to my side, Darren grabbed the broom. "What is it with you and vases?" He shouldered me aside to clean up the mess, but I didn't bother to answer him.

My hands shook and my eyes watered. My lungs expanded and contracted in rapid succession to the point that I might pass out. Darren was saying something to me, but the blood pounding in my ears drowned out his words. All I could see in my mind's eye were the red letters on the card written in a flourished script.

'See you soon, V.'

ABOUT THE AUTHOR

Erin Bedford is an otaku, recovering coffee addict, and Legend of Zelda fanatic. Her brain is so full of stories that need to be told that she must get them out or explode into a million screaming chibis. Obsessed with fairy tales and bad boys, she hasn't found a story she can't twist to match her deviant mind full of innuendos, snarky humor, and dream guys.

On the outside, she's a work from home mom and bookbinger. One the inside, she's a thirteen-year-old boy screaming to get out and tell you the pervy joke they found online. As an ex-computer programmer, she dreams of one day combining her love for writing and college credits to make the ultimate video game!

Until then, when she's not writing, Erin is devouring as many books as possible on her quest to have the biggest book gut of all time. She's written over thirty books, ranging from paranormal romance, urban fantasy, and even scifi romance.

Come chat me up!
www.erinbedford.com
Facebook.com/erinbedfordauthor
Instagram.com/erinbedfordauthor
twitter.com/erin_bedford
tiktok.com/@erinbedfordauthor